Miserations

Mike Gutowski

An extraterrestrial visited this world long ago and realized "this place needs a serious restoration". Time passed but the thought faded. Light years later, an ancestor of the same extraterrestrial who previously made the journey visited, looked around, and reached the same conclusion. Then left.

Opening the Plastic Wrap

<u>Social Obligations</u> 12/17/2022

Those chained to the throne tend to become servants of the throne.

<u>Lones</u> 12/18/2022 12:28 PM

He walked the lonely lane. Tried his best and kept no home. If today brings sorrow again, maybe light really isn't his friend.

Oh, he walked the lonely lane. Searched for comfort alone. Now he sees the lonely tree. He didn't adjust in time to otherwise be.

<u>Result Assault</u> 12/24/2022 09:09 PM

Every moment is born of a seed fertilized by a thought, word, or deed and sometimes grown by virtue of all three, blessed or cursed unto a living result free.

<u>Parent Lessons</u> 03/18/2023 12:48 PM

Dad was pretty smart. He achieved what he needed to survive. In youth, always the life experiments. Dipping his foot into the social pool. Found what he needed to succeed. Prospered enough to survive, then eventually thrive.

Mom suffered too many hard knocks in life, starting at a very young age. Those knocks swarmed like demons around her for the remainder of her life. Still, she taught much about how to survive amidst difficult circumstances.

We learned as best we could from each Star point.

<u>Thinking Exhaustion</u> 04/29/2023 01:32 PM

It's always somethin' somethin'. Somethin' to mourn. Somethin' to laugh about. Somethin' to scorn. Somethin' to worry about. Somethin' to bore. Somethin' to cry about. Somethin' more. Somethin' to count. Somethin' to score. Somethin' to shout about. Somethin' to roar. Somethin' to race. Somethin' to hit. Somethin' to chase. Somethin' to spit. Somethin' to care about. Somethin' to ring.

<u>Vague Acorns</u> 06/28/2023 09:01 AM

The vagaries of nicety have somehow eluded me.

<u>The End</u> 07/06/2023 06:33 AM

These rambles in the brambles have ended as all thoughts. When dreams must, in a final death, cough at thought closure coffins. Repose forever until the rotting runs the course.

Shots and Donuts

<u>Citizen Pool</u> 07/16/2023 09:27 AM

Government doesn't exist as ruler. It is imbued with a singular purpose: to serve the citizen. When government asserts itself, without consent, then the role of singular citizens becomes to dissolve the forces of government. Abort the government virus, then birth a reformed or more obedient government.

<u>Big Head</u> 07/16/2023 10:05 AM

The bigger the brain, the more likely the possibility of a Hollywood-style chamber of horrors concealed. Evil deeds mementos.

<u>Upper Lip Stink</u> 07/16/2023 11:35 AM

A moment exists as a past, present, and future pastry bun aroma.

<u>Order is Restraint</u> 07/16/2023 10:05 PM

Folds onto itself, does order, until the pains of restraint become a burden intellectual. All answers bevy heavy as speculations.

<u>Graffiti Ville</u> 07/19/2023 01:01 AM

Hand coded and painted wall signs illustrate where to obtain illicit drugs, booze, or call girls anyone's mind and body desires, but there's a fee for every visit including a use tax.

<u>Crunching</u> 07/19/2023 02:41 AM

Analyzing isn't understanding. Crunching numbers can be learned if enough effort is exerted. An understanding of the resulting answer may never become learned, or worse, the utility of the result is vehemently rejected when the frustrated learner refuses to accept the answer or answers. Such is the conflict of the human mind. Accept easy morals. Reject stressful ones. Answers involve decisions. The reality crunching then actually starts in a different form.

Helplessly Helpless 07/23/2023 03:31 AM

Why does this attractive woman want to make love to me? I'm not very good at it, nor terribly attractive. Didn't even shower today.

Tute (as in Prosti-) 07/23/2023 04:23 AM

Is she a cute tute, concerned of your needs mental and physical, or just a one-track mind harlot. Makes a difference. Marks boundaries. Sharpens the cliff's edge. Facilitates the rise and fall of Rome. In one sordid, smelly night.

Real Stuffing 07/24/2023 08:16 AM

There are consequences for delaying a realization of reality because reality won't be denied. It refuses such a rejection, with a vengeance accordingly.

Searches 07/30/2023 06:52 PM

The hardest thing to find in life isn't god. It's truth.

<u>Worry</u> 07/30/2023 06:58 PM

Don't worry about life. After all, life doesn't worry about us.

<u>On Beach Reading</u> 07/31/2023 03:20 PM

The first few pages of any books should focus our minds until the clothes hung in the closet are blown off their hangers and hooks. Worth the effort they are, every few pages, to take relief and allow the barbecue sauce to marinate a sweet belief. Reel in those needs from the weeds absent reluctance until ideas explode like a star's luminescence. Worth the effort to this end, or leave early and wonder just what lurked around the bends of essence.

Cheers? Leers? Jeers? Fears? Tears? Mends? Trends? Rants? Fends? Keep turnin' fan. The skin begs of air waves.

If I've taken you down to the white beach lined ocean, the oncoming waves between curious toe pokes of the water's reach, then my job is done, at least for a few weeks. Can't neglect that Guinness Blonde or Yuengling Traditional Lager for too long. Else boredom will call out to my female mates mane. A juicier orange always reimagined, of the flip flop clop or sandals mop, or the beach fries and vinegar gravy stand shop. Treks on and along the sun heated boardwalk planks lined of wide eyes in skulls readied for the taste of fish meat. At night, the sounds along such a journey echo a darkness of ocean crests. Another heaven day done, but always too soon. Go to bed, rest, as another day croons.

<u>Razors Edge</u> 07/31/2023 03:33 PM

Hot razors dig a notch into anyone's heart while suspecting a mates body moving further form a clear mental picture start, seeking malcontents to better knowns, and moments of illicit encounters. The imagination serves as a cruel head.

<u>On Personal Wars</u> 08/01/2023 12:36 AM

Is the individual person or nation better off at peace? Mutual needs determine such a circumstance. If a common goal intercedes, such as raising a family, or preserving a country's welfare begs for the high ground, then by all means peace must prevail. But when a passionate greed or lust jousts for possession of lands or domination of souls, these tasks are essentially defeated by all reason. Hell ascends on that part of a planet while reason treads a fast retreat.

On Rattlers 08/01/2023 01:13 PM

Call us whatever you want. You are do-nothings. Collecting paychecks from our wallets and banks. Equal justice under the law be damned. Crooks and do-nothings only deserve an end. The quicker the better.

Morning Foodie 08/01/2023 02:04 PM

We've got these choices. Go out and eat breakfast with me. We prepare and cook breakfast for us. Become breakfast for each other.

Utility 08/01/2023 02:26 PM

We're becoming older and more useless except for our own needs.

To Bee 08/01/2023 02:34 PM

Like all living things, they take over all they can, for sustenance and control. A sentient balance quotient remains flexible yet elusive.

Frenzy 08/01/2023 02:36 PM

Get out of my head! You words and thoughts! I must sometimes eat and shower my body in order to continue. If you fill my head too much, then my mind may explode and make you homeless amidst the universe's ether.

Advise Advisory 08/01/2023 03:25 PM

Many people will offer life advice they never followed, using you as a test ground, or purposefully misleading you into a revolving door of failure so you never exceed "them".

Dark Light 08/03/2023 04:50 PM

I'll take small and probe over large and hope any day.

Data Usage 08/05/2023 04:05 PM

Is this good or bad? I don't know. My perspective when reviewing my phone's Data Usage report. Another unsolved mystery courtesy of the Big Tech era.

Autumn 08/05/2023 04:21 PM

When life completes the cycle and dissolves into a winter fold.

Wham 08/07/2023 02:10 AM

There's no comfort in truth.

Sex Tears 08/07/2023 02:47 AM

During her orgasm he noticed streaks form, from the corners of her eyes, then tears began in a long line flow. He wondered if her winces served as alarms, not of anguish, but bliss. He later cried a bit much over the thought of it.

Perspective Retrospective 08/07/2023 09:29 AM

Willfully blind or blindingly willful?

Drops and Tears 08/08/2023 04:14 AM

So many women. So many tears. So many men. So many fears.

On New 08/08/2023 01:46 PM

New exists on a frequency variable. Doesn't usually mean better. It's just some or other clown show trying to take over the circus.

Real and Real 08/10/2023 01:05 AM

The guy who works on a project at home and happens to see a very sexy woman neighbor in her backyard who continuously woos no one in particular with sexy words and clothes worn and dances sexual maneuvers. The guy's project is going to hell.

Only Destruction 08/10/2023 01:45 AM

To restart one must first shut down.

A Life 08/10/2023 03:20 PM

Roller coaster, Ferris wheel, Merry-go-round, Freak show.

Den 08/11/2023 11:40 AM

This place is a space of books and Thrace. It serves as mind to drudgery and lace.

Adult Life Lesson #1 08/11/2023 02:13 PM

Never run out of coffee, smokes, and toilet tissue. To do so tempts an Ultimate Doom guest appearance upon life's center stage.

Hail the O 08/12/2023 12:24 PM

Many small words renting the letter "o" bookmarked by consonants flow out easy between the lips.

<u>Grief of Love</u> 08/13/2023 09:18 PM

When we were first introduced she seemed to show real interest in him. He felt flattered, so he sought to spend more time in her company of moments. As he grew to know her better, the intrigue monitor became quite stimulated. They grew together in the company of each other until his own fears of inadequacy caused him to desist and step back from the relationship.

The look on her face at this retraction of budding, soon blooming love would never be forgotten by each. Their hearts mutually sunk in unison. She stunned him deeply with that look. Her eyes said it all. Her face froze in grief he had never seen previously, not even at a funeral.

From that moment forward he regretted allowing his own insecurities to get the best of him. A single moment in time that could never be erased.

<u>Marketers</u> 08/15/2023 08:57 PM

Should spend all of your time going here and there, buying stuff, making new friends, socializing with Democrats and Liberals and leftists and blah, blah, blah bullinski.

<u>Skeeterville</u> 08/15/2023 10:47 PM

I've donated blood to the mosquito population more times than remembrance allows. At a welding rods factory; at a steel wire spooling factory; at a cardboard box manufacturing facility. The world surrounding mosquitos serves as a blood buffet banquet.

<u>Marketeers</u> 08/16/2023 06:53 AM

They are called Influencers now. Laughable to me, as age tells me they were the talky sheisters of years ago selling anything and everything that moved, and some that barely moved, if at all. Basically, people who help people in time of mutual greed circumstances.

<u>To Be or Not To Be</u> 08/18/2023 08:31 PM

Not supposed to be here. Just a pulse carrier, now. Sometimes it is lost, hiding, yet breaths of air betray an existence in tow. Works okay. Adjustments made day to day.

<u>Jeopardy, Category Is Robot Poop</u> 08/20/2023 08:31 PM

Answer: What is the 21st century?

Pretty Eyes 08/21/2023 12:01 AM

Pretty Eyes and An Ugly Soul, a concert as common as a performance of Towering Old Oaktree and The Carpenter Ants featuring The Woodpecker. Bangs a death drum beat prance.

All I Know 08/21/2023 12:31 AM

Sound, truth, tears for years and years, appreciated for a fitting purpose.

Wall Wacks 08/21/2023 02:15 AM

It wasn't her wisdom sharing he objected to. It was the manner in which she expressed it. Demeaning. Overbearing, like the erratic swing of a sledge hammer into a plaster wall covering cinderblocks. Coarse, chaotic, sometimes cruel in reverberations.

Bristle 08/21/2023 04:56 AM

He really wished he could get her out of his soul, but thoughts of shared experiences with her were still stuck between the teeth like a single broken toothbrush bristle.

Bullshit 08/21/2023 03:27 PM

There are too many humans who have bullshit running through their veins. Maybe climate can correct.

<u>Commercials</u> 08/21/2023 03:30 PM

The more they scream the less credible they seem.

<u>EV and Salad</u> 08/21/2023 03:35 PM

All the gov needs to do is shut down the energy grid to stick you like a pig. Yet, the same gov monsters push EV's on us daily. Gas fueled vehicles meant travel and transport freedom for over 100 years. Think about it. The woke crowd chanters and chaos mongers, while eating their salads and dried crickets, may mistake our ignorance of their enlightenment as acceptance.

<u>Somnambulant Escape Patterns</u> 08/20/2023 03:37 PM

Save the climate, choke the woke. Save the government, choke the woke. Save a soul, choke the woke. What a horrible dream.

<u>Dopey</u> 08/21/2023 03:40 PM

Go woke means go broke.

Political Math 08/21/2023 04:12 PM

Democrat traitors are patriots. Republican patriots are traitors. See Joe Biden Philadelphia speech.

Politics 08/21/2023 04:17 PM

Select lying gone wild.

Empire 08/22/2023 01:55 PM

The deceits of one may seal the fates of many others. We may be flies, but swarms we call, if we must.

Climate Cuckoo 08/22/2023 02:24 PM

All you liberals who speak so wise, suicide yourselves to save our lives.

On Spiders 08/23/2023 03:09 AM

Old houses house numerous types of spiders and memories. Spiders, like memories, tend to make a surprise appearance. A few examples may suffice. The spindly, quarter-sized momma either located at in or out of way spaces, spins a web in high room corners, in a bathroom's dark places, near windows on the outside or inside especially near tree limbs, and at all available spaces of front or back porch locations. The little but speedy coal black spiders, high jumpers, favor dusty environs under bed frames, behind bookcases and bedroom furniture. The large black spiders like airy environs like just above ceiling fans, in attic corners where the wind accesses entry, and in the wooded areas between floors and ceilings. Each grouping seems to have been born with a roadmap to success when it comes to tempting other inhabitants of the insect and bug worlds. Active at night, absent during daylight, by and large except for vacant and wavy remnants of the spun night traps. Each day's web remnants hold memories.

<u>Much Shadows</u> 08/24/2023 04:19 PM

It ain't much, but any ain't much is still somethin'.

<u>Time Dilation</u> 08/24/2023 10:33 PM

So, I see a religion commercial referring to 70 AD. The speaker talks like he knows what humans thought in 70 AD. Just a minute ago I watched a news reporter spout on and on about a political crime. I know. The garbage dump seems always open.

<u>Political Chicanery</u> 08/25/2023 09:13 AM

There's no such thing as a "political" crime, but the media reporter thinks such a crime is real. Such stupidity infects like a virus in the 21st century.

The Five Tenets 08/25/2023 10:58 PM

In this century, one must believe and learn:

> The climate is God.
> Learn, know, and use the proper pronouns.
> Humans can biologically change gender.
> Socializing means never instigate a micro-aggression.
> All of your problems were caused by others, not you.

None of these tenets is grounded in a single grain of truth.

Sometimes 08/26/2023 07:00 AM

Get what you need before you need what you want.

On Eating 08/28/2023 01:53 AM

Before going to sleep, while lying in bed, he would review what foods and drinks were consumed from 12:01 AM until 11:59 PM. Healthy? Tasty?

Bland? Too expensive? Too cheap, robbing of a pleasant flavor?

<u>Happy No Matter What</u> 08/28/2023 02:04 AM

Oh, that is just so much fun. Yes, it is.

<u>How does "this" work</u> 08/28/2023 02:08 AM

What is the "this" seldom remains a mystery to the nefarious thinker, but remains a mystery to the audible listener.

<u>On Skin</u> 08/28/2023 02:11 AM

We don't pay much attention to our skin unless others can see it. It itches. It stings, but a by passer's observations may demonstrate fear of the skin trekker.

<u>Moments</u> 08/28/2023 02:13 AM

Any 3 or 4 something time in the morning feels like a lonely and scary place. Alone in near silence does an oddity to the brain.

<u>Caverns</u> 08/28/2023 02:18 AM

The women in his mind from birth until now haunted the mind difficult.

Ruler of the Body 08/28/2023 02:20 AM

The mind should rule the body, but it is the other way around for much of the populace. Comfort is routinely sought physically and mentally. Comfort is a demon fool and nitpicker, much like a chihuahua.

Au Terrible 08/28/2023 02:29 AM

The terrible is the norm in too many places.

Moth Life 08/28/2023 02:29 AM

It is difficult to get through a day without adhering to someone's schedule. This flitting most. Seriously.

Toilet Treachery 08/28/2023 02:46 AM

My toilet began automatically flushing one evening, unexpectedly. At first I wondered how it could be so. I lived alone. So, I went and fiddled to the sound, lifted the tank top, observed the water refusing to refill, and the water flow stopper remain up as if suspended in animation. I inspected the stopper, water level lever, and small chain connected to the exterior flush lever. All seemed fine. I manually pushed down the stopper, and the tank refilled. Befuddled by a circumstance never encountered before, I shut the bathroom door, walked a few steps distance to the bedroom, then shut that door for time to recover from the episode. The silence became eerie. Proceeded to attempt a relaxation moment, but dang it, such moments had fled town like an expelled traveler. My evening silence had been stolen. Then, the toilet flushed again. I repeated the previous process after exiting the bed. I was able to make some chain and lever modifications using varied twists and turns of each mechanism. Went back to bed, and again the toilet flushed. "Ghosts in the system," I morosely thought. For 8 months I listened to repeated flushing, every 70 seconds or so, because the local hardware store didn't carry the flush stopper mechanism that would fit my toilet. I ordered one from them, and they said it was on back order and they would let me know when it arrived. I checked time and again. No positive results for the order. Unfortunately, more disaster awaited. The government water bill, 10 times higher than the average bill previously received. I appealed the charges with the County government office and the appeal was denied. I paid the bill, courtesy of a $10-dollar unavailable flush stopper (basically a rounded, flat piece of rubber slightly larger than a silver dollar). Eventually, I drained a second toilet in the house, and turned the water valve to "off" position to prevent the refilling phase, then I purged it of the working flush stopper and used it for the toilet near the bedroom.

<u>August Repeat</u> 08/28/2023 03:00 AM

It's August in the States. The usual hot mess of high humidity and heat, sprinkled in with varied thunderstorms and lightning strikes, sometimes peppered with tornado watches. I haven't used the air conditioning (A/C) since last August except for the days my youngest daughter visited and stayed. Still trying to make financial ends meet after the toilet flush stopper fiasco.

<u>Cities</u> 08/28/2023 01:40 PM

If your last or current mayor ruled and preened over the dark comedy of murder, rape, child trafficking, and more chaos, one must conclude the citizens of such a city, generally, are pukes tossing votes out for chump change favors, permitting themselves to remain, almost completely defenseless by common law, and thus worthy of the honorable and daily beatings they suffer.

Envy Scurrilous 08/28/2023 02:05 PM

Younger people don't like or much tolerate older people because the young people know the older people have earned the benefits of experience. Such a benefit cannot be cheated upon to make a passing grade. Old people knowledge and experience perspectives stings the minds of younger people.

Education Theft 08/28/2023 05:59 PM

Teachers today are intent on stealing kids' minds. That's crookery. That's unhealthy.

Age Conundrum 08/28/2023 11:01 PM

I don't miss being young, or inexperienced, or unable to properly assess what is good or bad, safe or dangerous, right or wrong, moral or immoral.

Grown Cold 08/29/2023 11:59 AM

Reminiscing is nice but reliving it is not so much.

Politics and Climate 08/29/2023 05:59 PM

Climate suggestion box: Climate have your way with a corrupt deadly politician.

Demon Signs 08/29/2023 06:20 PM

Politicians demonize the people who don't buy into politician lies. Politician liars equal destructive demons. Let us help you means let us control you; to negatively exploit your trust. False trust is born of lies.

Lyin' Eyes and Ears 08/29/2023 06:56 PM

Those who regularly lie consider the lies to be told their own moral imperative. Evil, evil, evil.

Fear the Free 08/29/2023 06:58 PM

Politicians are lucky we don't brandish weapons against them. Their gun policies reflect such a fear. Those policies also provide immutable truth they don't really give a rat's ass what happens to us.

Grave Reflections 08/29/2023 06:59 PM

Eventually we'll all become grave diggers.

Linguistics 08/29/2023 10:02 PM

He's skilled at interpreting bleeped language.

Shit Turds 08/29/2023 10:21 PM

The word combination "shit turd" implied folly frailty, but in the city he resided such a word salad was served up early and often amidst the neighborhood.

Squares 08/30/2023 02:14 AM

If square one is unknowing, then square two is asked a question. Can't get answers to questions not asked, but the answered questions are still devoid of some times, many times an intentional effect created by the answer. Ain't that a load of shit. Must then be ruminated.

Aging 08/30/2023 02:34 AM

The last thing you remember tends to be the first thing forgotten.

Planet Aquanet 08/30/2023 02:38 AM

If your flooring, either rug, wood, or tile, is mysteriously accumulating hairballs, then your home friend is likely a cat. If you don't share a home with a cat, then an alien invasion instituted by the Aquanet planetary system has likely commenced.

Insanity Sanity 08/30/2023 08:09 PM

It sometimes remains impossible to maintain a position as one of the few sane sentient humans in this world. The spiteful and resentful have taken over en masse.

Fire Fables 08/31/2023 02:25 PM

What is lost in the memory may still never be forgotten.

Life Line 08/31/2023 04:16 PM

I don't want to live forever. I just want to live long enough.

Calm Windless 08/31/2023 04:29 PM

Only moments comfortable. Only moments.

On A Beginning Point 09/02/2023 02:45 PM

Pissing is a much too frequent regular occurrence for old me. The moments of the flow do offer some contemplation time. And thus, this book was born and now presented before interested reader minds. A simple piss as hit or miss still remains a mystery of time and space. Many scientific elements stream emitted in the process of these actions. How the human mind works philosophic, zoetic.

Life isn't beautiful. It is more observed than tolerated. Adjusted to while seeking a safe space in accordance with the definitions and uses for the individual mind residing inside of it.

Which leads into the crazy and crazier matters of religion, marketing, and politicians as interpreted by people. Such commiserations ignobly serve as enmity traps.

Here we are in the 21st Century. Still questioning what it means to be human, a human. Time now. Time set.

<u>On Liberals, Leftists, and Conservatives</u>
09/03/2023 12:55 PM

After the apocalypse, politically, the only survivors cling to one of three groups of political theories: libs, lefties, and cons.

A meeting was convened, and in conference, the proceedings went as follows.

Libs claimed conservatives cause harm by not following lib life maintenance theory. The cons claimed leave us alone, we don't bother anyone. The lefties advocated compromise.

Compromise reached, and the resulting societal construct was determined as leftists monitored enforcement of laws imposed by liberals.

All citizens were mandated to live in glass bubbles, squares, or rectangles. Law violations reported by liberals were reviewed by leftists who then authorized the extent and degree of violation punishments. The usual punishment involved a release of an invisible spray by the liberals upon law violators' habitats. The spray punishment usually resulted in death of the inhabitants. Gradually, no more cons existed.

Cages 09/03/2023 01:56 PM

Some humans, a majority, seek order, the sweet scent of it, sentience of a common ground existence. Others, a minority, seek chaos. They fear order, consider it a cage.

Hoax World News 09/03/2023 08:07 PM

Virtually every media story published in web media is either a hoax or flat out lie. Seems to be written by 5th grade elementary school creative writing class level of humans. These wonderful teachers need a raise, or a death sentence imposed on their careers. A raise for Hollywood worthy garbage scripts. A death sentence for their propagandist careers.

<u>Night Moths, Crickets, and Darkness Unknown</u>
09/03/2023 08:42 PM

They fly like spies, crawl like Navy Seals, in movements mysterious, but of purposeful mystery.

A trio of moths danced around a wooden electric line pole in a seeming pre-ordained mating ritual. A grounded group of crickets cautiously moved closer to the event. Such moments are spurred on, ignited by an evening sky of varied visible star Constellations. Sky patterns are so designated by human imaginations. A story awaits, a tale telling.

I, night traveler in the evening light of the backyard, ventured to view a waning gibbous Blue Moon three-quarters full; a last and alone night moth still dancing amongst the electric pole wires; a spider weaving a web only visual form a certain angle glowing in moon rays; a solo sound of a cricket's violin concerto; and a moment's deal broken as a beige Gojira-sized cockroach raced across the hard cement walkway across abutting the grassy yard's surface like an Indy car racing on the oval.

One of the body brown wings white moths sat upon a lawn chair next to the one where I reclined. We had a brief chat while I smoked a little cigar. I say chat, because it moved tiny head to look at me from another angled perspective. A good listener. Neve said a word. Patient one, too. I went back into the house. An hour later looked out the window again and spotted the moth sitting atop the lawn chair I had previously vacated.

<u>Body Lost</u> 09/04/2023 01:22 PM

Lost the idea while in bathroom. Can't even resurrect it. The body of thought then disappeared.

<u>Bee in the Backyard</u> 09/04/2023 02:39 PM

Bee on a walking two-day bender. Saw it two days ago. Now walking wobbly on the cemented back yard floor. Spreads the wings but can't manage a takeoff. I said some kind, encouraging words. Wondered if it sucked some plants poisonous nectar. Many plants and flowers bloom in this yard and neighboring yards. Perhaps sipped too much sap from the flowers nearby?

Truth Bomb 09/05/2023 07:23 AM

Humans hide from the truth because it can hurt them. The ugly truth is pretty as hell.

Advanced Age 09/05/2023 10:39 AM

Means the body plays a game of Monopoly to select which body joints to land on, then buys houses of pain to take up lodging.

Humans are Animals 09/06/2023 10:31 AM

Damn the government doom dogs.

Perspective 09/06/2023 01:07 PM

A human's demons take a difficult long time during attempts to achieve perspective.

Elitism 09/07/2023 11:04 AM

It's a world where the elites rule everything. Displease them and suffer the consequences. Big Tech serves the elitest servitude model.

Teachers 09/07/2023 11:15 AM

First, it was we'll mold your mind to think like us. Now, it is we'll mold your body to look like us.

Time Limits 09/07/2023 12:13 PM

All things exist temporary in this world, including this world itself.

Addiction Tastes 09/07/2023 12:19 PM

Make the coffee. Drink the coffee. Piss the coffee.

Squatters Defense 09/07/2023 12:27 PM

The house invited me in.

Car Purchase Anxiety 09/07/2023 12:29

Many of the past few days of posts reflect a car buyers philosophical predicament challenges. So, if exists a need to tap into inner fears, then commence the car purchase process. Rid oneself of a crumpled tech machine in exchange for a less crumpled one.

Burning Man Festival 09/07/2023 12:32 PM

In many cities, every day is burning man desecration.

Obsessions 09/07/2023 12:34 PM

Time is relative. Thoughts of time are relevant.

<u>Connections</u> 09/07/2023 12:35 PM

Finding a place to live and die is a great and momentous life's quest.

<u>On Writing</u> 09/07/2023 12:38 PM

Writer's block isn't a curse. The curse is the writer's writing. Once the writers start writing the thoughts have ignited like a brain bomb.

<u>Daily Reflections</u> 09/07/2023 12:47 PM

Is that a poppy seed or a mouse turd?

<u>Ancient's Wisdom</u> 09/07/2023 02:22 PM

Infatuation. Great Ceaser's ghost.

<u>New York Stylings</u> 09/07/2023 02:23 PM

The accent drives the air like an ear punch.

<u>Chaos Theory</u> 09/07/2023 03:52 PM

Any business, government officials, or individual who bases life affecting decisions on their personal opinion, and absolutely and intentionally ignores the rule of law and common-sense humanity standards exemplifies the chaos in all of our cities.

Their simple rule is keeping the chaos moving forward.

<u>Lies Leaders</u> 09/07/2023 06:06 PM

In no particular order: politicians, religionists, used car salespeople, scientists, doctors, lawyers, teachers.

<u>The Library</u> 09/09/2023 11:37 PM

Always treated the local library as a supernatural entity, what with so many books, many exuding a pleasant odor pushing out titles that remind me of favorite candies. Rich textures; pleasant aromas; daring in scent; mysteries revealed at the turn of a page.

The most momentous moment of such a personal affair came during the revelations exposed while stroking the binding and covers front and back. What mysteries, deep thoughts, scandalous secrets would be undressed? A restless urge for reveal in minds young to old.

Imagined there existed, hidden, electronic monitors amidst the bookshelves, such devices creating waves of muffled sounds to the ear, but still a means of coaxing the intrepid yet curious of heart to in fact open the book, using a delicate rub of fingers upon the cover as pretext to a most pleasant, anticipated mind ejaculation, as a read of the words tasted when filtered through the brain. Blindness, deafness of all library sounds and echoes disappeared instantly.

More modern libraries, tech enhanced, might observe the pleasures bestowed upon readers in comfortable chairs, couches, floors, readied for a reader's insatiable desires of literary consumption.

The Librarian served as monitor, crafter of search success, checking on the comfort and purpose of the crowd in attendance. One by one the Librarian spied, judged, searched and found purpose ascertained. I will not describe the Librarian except to say an enabler of intellectual desires. Much experienced in helping those desires to become fulfilled.

I myself heard the Librarian whisper, in a voice that tingled my veins, a question on that specific morning. "Why is there an unknown biological presence in this place today?" The Librarian's gazed had spotted me. Stunned, I failed to respond. I wanted to respond, but I'd already been captured by the first few pages of the book already opened. Perhaps a mystery previously solved in one of the thousands of books lining the aisles of shelving.

Mercurial Rant 09/12/2023 03:56 PM

Evey human, humanoid harbors a dickhead or cunt buried inside the personality box. Some set it free too often and either suffer consequences or reap benefits, depending on the social or business situation. Assisted by corrupt media propaganda. The words "honest media" qualifies as an oxymoron comparable to "honest politician".

Tete a Tetris 09/12/2023 04:02 PM

Politicians and media wrongfully stoke a dousing of our life, liberty, and pursuit of happiness, so we sacrificed them to the climate gods.

Hedge Hoggin' 09/12/2023 04:38 PM

Just hedge hoggin' along, one earthbound day at a time.

Mist Pickles 09/12/2023 04:43 PM

As I've aged, gained a more prescient opinion regarding the taste and texture of pickles. Delicious.

<u>State Veracity</u> 09/12/2023 04:47 PM

The State likes to proffer their ability to keep safe the streets and homes of citizens, but when push comes to shove, the State begs off on the responsibility they claim. BTW, in more than a few States, the primary responsibility for self-protection rests in the citizens.

States like to ignore that earned right in order to stomp out such a constitutional notion. Citizens should lawfully be trained how to use self-defense weapons. Every society in history has risen or fallen depending on the fate of self-defense rights. The evidence lives everywhere. Just look around. The State regularly turns a blind eye towards violent and even petty crimes. Begs off on any such responsibility.

Otherwise, the State is a dog that won't hunt, trot, or run towards danger, or riotous activity. But the State sure runs towards fine foods, wines, and other scrumptious edibles.

Madness Views 09/15/2023 10:04 AM

Evil lives in the mind of the contemplator. A battle ensues daily, everywhere.

Content 09/15/2023 10:07 AM

Hear me whether you believe it or not.

Nonsense 09/15/2023 10:11 AM

Selling stale ideas to nonsensical hungry minds.

Societal Constructs 09/17/2023 05:38 PM

There exists religious cults, which are all of them. There exists political cults, which are all of them. The game is just as you've learned it, imbedded into young brains so deeply by education cults. The young learners almost never learn objective truths.

Apparently, it's more important to learn societal rules than it is to learn math and history and reading. Those educational quality exceptions are generally only gifted to those powerful of influence capabilities. They learn propaganda programmed rules of society, but so too exist numerous rules following exceptions. In other words, wealthy elites live by a separate set of laws and rules. The rich get what they want on demand, a choice as effective as a button click of the remote-control streaming device.

Money speaks a different language amongst different societal classes. Give it up to the totalitarian elites or suffer the negative consequences of your derision. No job. No shelter. No food. No life. A truth fate miserable to consider for the masses not elites.

<u>Majic Book</u> 09/19/2023 03:07 PM

There's a book, ancient in origin, which provides social, cultural, and religious tenets as means for the reader to ascend into a better, more palatable human entity. Regurgitate as needed.

<u>Stupid is as Stupid does</u> 09/19/2023 07:08 PM

It's the era of stupid, and stupid is winning in a landslide.

<u>Scamicals</u> 09/19/2023 07:08 PM

Upon further thought we found another scam to be exploited. Soon to be made into a Broadway theater play. Perhaps, a musical.

Mission Shadows 09/20/2023 12:42 AM

Every church harbors a secret, and every secret requires a destination.

Circles 09/21/2023 03:52 AM

Immortals can die. Infinity is not infinite.

Deadly Lies 09/21/2023 11:34 PM

Lies espoused by journalist and politicians, as means to denigrate and direct actions violent against the innocent must be stopped, by elimination of those murderous of mind liars.

AI Lifestyles 09/21/2023 11:48 PM

Odds are high the most corrupt political parties will register AI beings to vote until they are caught doing so and then recruit media acolytes to promote an apology registered as an accident or mistake.

Futurism 09/21/2023 11:56 PM

Guessing humans exist who have discovered methods to see the future, and learned skills to influence the proceedings there.

Political Mouthers 09/25/2023 03:58 PM

Way too many mouth sheisters out there. They shout inane and nefarious threats, forgetting their birth rights conveniently.

<u>Unstoppable (Story Idea)</u> 09/26/2023 11:16 AM

Once he knows who did it, he becomes unstoppable.

The cancer had gotten the best of him. The eyes of the doctors and nurses told him so in wordless expressions. He thought of a suicide ending during the treatments process, but never settled on the poetic, representative method and conclusion satisfactory. The expressions and impressions of this world would still persist. Thoughts of his children enforced a positive demeanor upon the soul. Memories of raising and educating them reinforced his will to survive and thrive.

He learned to better use senses imbued upon humans at birth; called forth efforts to better understand these gifts; use them as means to sharpen perspectives and anticipations of danger.

The names of the aggrandizers of a peaceful world in favor of chaos are not important. Their actions must be stopped cold, at any cost, to prevent a life of misery and regret. Misery real, a truth inescapable; and regret haunting for an absence of past self-defense actions. The worst, and best, is yet to come. On balance, a result is uncertain.

Partnership 09/27/2023 04:21 AM

Be kind, respectful, understanding, tolerant, and reliable stewards of each other's needs.

Time Times 09/30/2023 12:46 PM

Seconds of time take time, taking our time.

Selective Relevant Efficiency 09/30/2024 01:55 PM

The time is mine. Only I can take responsibility for how and when it is used for actions other than breathing.

Moments Peace 09/30/2023 09:24

No longer chasing moments. Those moments don't care.

Success Level 10/01/2023 10:29 AM

I wish your successes to be so great in number and feat that you will never suffer the need of my help.

<u>Listens</u> 10/01/2023 10:51 AM

Poor listeners hear what they want to hear. Good listeners hear what they fear to hear.

<u>Un-gifts</u> 10/01/2023 10:57 AM

If my dignity is taken, may it curse the taker.

<u>Unknown Chapter</u> 10/02/2023 09:22 PM

At the height of the fight when all seemed lost and retreat loomed necessary, fighter who had previously died had sparked back into existence. Fighters from this world and unknown worlds, and fighters from varied time frame eras past, present, and future. A magician who could summon meteors and asteroids, then directed their fragments like bullets ignited or spears hurled. Four-legged animals and two-legged creatures of varied sizes, and large shiny machines of locomotive methods not visible, moved around on the ground and some hovered above it, carried warriors able to fire long metal weapons which ejected projectiles into skin, limbs, and bodies. Some of the machines revealed no visible drivers yet still moved around.

The projectiles broke the bodies of fighters in varied areas of impact. Shiney weapons of slippery integrity ejected smoke and flames sending flammable liquids pools in varied directions creating fires upon the ground touched.

He turned around after a loud sound to see what menace had arrived from behind, able to commit such devastating damage. No leader of these horrors showed itself. He turned again to gaze upon the battlefield lands and noticed missing were the heaps of broken bodies of human, humanoid, creatures, and perhaps other-worldly demons, but he couldn't see them now as the wind had changed and laid down a thick white smoke from weapons discharges like a covering blanket.

Through his boot soles he felt ground tremors first slow in frequency, then faster and louder, until the ground heaved and swayed like ocean waves. The irregular motions knocked him to the ground. Whizzing hoots from behind rolled his body to and fro. His breaths became captured in the violent storm of movements until a mind clearness faded and failed.

Awake again, he tried to revive from an unsteady sleep but remained unable to move. He guessed his body had become stuck in a muddy goo created by the preceding events. His head managed a slanted view of the battlefield grounds. What he saw defied description. No evidence remained of the events experienced by all of his senses.

<u>Calm</u> 10/03/2023 07:01 PM

Solitude is my solace.

<u>Exercise</u> 10/04/2023 01:37 PM

At my age, ripping up junk mail is a primary source of cardio.

<u>Mirrors</u> 10/06/2023 02:14 PM

We live in the age of a most prevalent two-way mirror.

<u>Madness</u> 10/06/2023 02:22 PM

There is a method to every last bit of madness. To think such a development is mere happenstance would be foolish.

<u>Run, Stop, Run</u> 10/08/2023 10:35 PM

They raced forward at breakneck speed trying to catch it sweet. So long and so hard their feet pounded the street. The journey lasted too many fortnights consecutive until a single thought crested the horizon. Perhaps what we chase is not out there somewhere just outside a grasp. Perhaps what we want, and need is somewhere else. To turn around seemed a waste of time.

Stop for a moment. Look deep inside. That mystery we seek creeps lonely there. It is the mystery we fear to face. The gift we chase resides in one place. Grasp it with one mind and make it take. Clear a path and rest in peace. The mystery lives in a single space we've owned, all along, but never faced.

<u>Catch-22</u> 10/10/2023 01:53 AM

Multi-tasking is a management curse. By the time you begin to work on the first task, the others fade from memory.

<u>Perspective Redux</u> 10/10/2023 03:34 AM

One person's thoughts and dreams may exist for another person as nightmares and screams.

Chocolate Milk 10/10/2023 03:39 AM

A nagging curse kicks like a mule. Walked to the grocery store but forgot to bring along my grocery list. In my head, I ran through the needed and some wanted items. I tried to stick the items in my brain with chewed memorization brain cell gum. "Buy chocolate milk." Reminded the noggin many times. Even shouted to the woodpecker in the distance hidden in the tree line. Entered the store, purchased items. Left the store, proud of myself, then realized, "next time-next time" remember to buy chocolate milk. Anyway, the bags were one less liquid item lighter.

Water Stains 10/10/2023 03:47 AM

The mind tends to beat itself up when reviewing (b)rain showers of past discretions and indiscretions.

Perspective Crucifixion 10/10/2023 03:53 AM

Tell me what you think. Fine. Tell me what to think. Go to hell.

City Life 10/10/2023 03:59 AM

The cities are filled with lamers, blamers, and framers living amidst some many blocks of sensible sanelings.

City Foibles 10/10/2023 04:07 AM

The efficiency of word use, and syllabic truncation gets a silence plus rating. Loud nonsense locations buzz like an angry wasp looking to unleash a harsh sting jab.

Liberty Food 10/10/2023 04:10 AM

Give me liberty or give me a chocolate covered donut or bagel. Death can wait.

Sane Lanes 10/10/2023 04:11 AM

Sanity is a relative sensation. Tingles insides, the moments of it.

Imagination Patch 10/10/2023 04:13 AM

Daydreams and nightmares exist like kissing cousins.

Vibrations 10/10/2023 04:16 AM

Worked a lot of night shifts in my younger years. 4 AM often stung the mind. Pierced the inner soul regions.

<u>Knuckle Stings</u> 10/10/2023 04:19 AM

For the author, a blank page turns into a bare-knuckled pugilistic bout. Write versus thoughts to merit a write. Readers serve as judges.

<u>Crazy Fare</u> 10/10/2023 04:22 AM

The problem with laws rests in the necessity to follow them. In every society, bar none, the politically connected or wealthy live permitted to buy favor as protection from the laws. So much for fairness. Fairness took the bargain priced last train to Crazytown.

<u>Human Mystery</u> 10/10/2023 04:33 AM

What do we really know about each other when we likely don't really know a whole hell of a lot about ourselves.

<u>Truth Rule</u> 10/11/2023 06:46 PM

There exists no simple means to commiserate with Truth. It stings while the sound of it enlightens. It literally kicks mind ass into, for some, enlightenment. To reject such enlightenment permits misery to dance free.

Immutable 10/13/2023 01:03 PM

The more power and influence one human/humanoid wields over another, generally, the less the former can be trusted. Exceptions rare.

Moo Juice 10/13/2023 01:59 PM

Fortunately, my body appreciates cow's milk. Life rolls along from beginning teats to ending teats.

Cigar Monarchy 10/13/23 02:05 PM

Why are cigar smoking moments more titillating then sex in any form? Further ruminations required.

Sub-thought: safer than sex? Potential results of cigar smoking versus potential results of sex poking.

On Alcohol 10/13/2023 02:09 PM

Beer is the poor human's wine.

Machine Tools 10/14/2023 06:10 AM

Hoping for a savior is how fools play the life game. Learn how to save yourself, then make the world a better place as a natural progression.

Sentient Somnambulance 10/14/2023 06:32 AM

It only takes a long time to get to know someone if you truly don't even know yourself.

Perspective Punches 10/14/2023 06:35 AM

Learning about monsters / creatures helps to achieve revelations about humans / humanoids.

Graphite Box Check 10/14/2023 06:39 AM

Do I have to explain everything or does everything have to explain me.

Loveless 10/14/2023 07:29 AM

Lost in love. Right. More like lost in greed.

Culture Crush 10/14/2023 07:31 AM

Monsters raised by monsters raising monsters. What could possibly go wrong?

Human Insanity 10/14/2023 08:19 AM

There's no such thing as a decent socialist or Marxist. They all want what you've earned, no questions asked.

There's no such thing as a moral elitest. See above.

<u>Whine Wine</u> 10/14/2023 08:25 AM

The wine class raises whiners.

<u>On Reading</u> 10/14/2023 08:35 AM

The more you read the less you need to read.

A well-practiced reader benefits from an ability to shut away the world outside, allowing the world inside the mind to flourish.

<u>Political Personal</u> 10/15/2023 09:06 PM

It's impossible to separate the political from the personal, and anyone who claims such an ability to do so is prejudicing the effort.

<u>On gods</u> 10/15/2023 10:09 PM

A god who talks in riddles isn't an all-knowing god. Just a physically powerful narcissist enjoying the chaos.

<u>On Business Acumen</u> 10/16/2023 12:31 PM

The favored employees working in every business are generally less productive, yet reap most of the benefits and credits due to management overseers' social preference privileges granted gratuitously. Nepotism and favoritism rules.

On Libturds 10/16/2023 01:46 PM

Perfectly willing to ban meat products but absolutely tolerant of bona fide terrorists.

Inter-Dimensions (Story) 10/16/2023 11:38 PM

A bridge links two adjacent dimension worlds. In one dimension are humanoids who evolved able to enter and exit each dimension. In the other dimension exists humans who can never leave theirs.

Human Inclinations 10/19/2023 02:40 AM

If you've ever loved hating something, or hated loving something, then take in that knowledge experience for just a moment. Realize that human/humanoid moment mentally. Explains a lot.

Biological Anomalies 10/17/2023 02:59 AM

Sad times rain tears, and happy times, too.

Error oh Error! 10/18/2023 09:38 PM

A doubt's hesitation tends to avoid crude mistakes. A certainty's immediate action tends to create rude mistakes.

On Women 10/18/2023 09:43 PM

A ... U ... Y ... W .... .

On Men 10/18/2023 09:43 PM

B ... P ... Z ... .

On Aging 10/18/2023 09:56 PM

Some sleeping humans are awakened by nightmares. Some humans are awakened by piss biology.

On Food Need 10/18/2023 09:59 PM

Prayers don't feed the hungry. Actions do.

Lie full Truths 10/20/2023 08:10 AM

We live in a world now where much life has grown to become a used car salesperson.

On Congress (Bullshit) Sensibility 10/20/2023 10:44 AM

Someone should get elected to serve the United States Congress, either chamber will do, and then, before starting their term, legally change their name to include every word and symbol in the New Websters Dictionary unabridged edition, so when called upon to speak about an issue while Congress is in session, all congressional madness will be stopped cold.

<u>Imagination Place</u> 10/22/2023 03:00 AM

Crossing over into the Real World from Imagination place is strictly prohibited, which explains why the occurrences are so frequent, for better or worse.

<u>On Washing Clothes</u> 10/22/2023 03:13 AM

I've always found a washing of my clothes a rather cleansing of the soul experience, required about once every two conventional months in time.

<u>On Politics</u> 10/22/2023 03:33 AM

Plenty to write or speak, but what's the point? Don't eat what can't be shit away.

Journal of Brain Sparks

<u>On Government Math</u> 10/22/2023 03:35 AM

Government audits never balance on purpose.

<u>On Ex-Spouses</u> 10/22/2023 03:35 AM

Wondered once what I'd say to my ex-wife if I ever saw her again. She'd likely make at least one snide remark about how I should do this or that. She always seemed to consider it her hobby to adjust something on me like clothing, or a facial expression like squinting. After all of this "no longer sharing the same space" time, I might say, "Don't adjust me. I'm no longer available in your province of control."

Perspectives Natural 10/22/2023 04:46 AM

How does the woman handle it? How does the man handle it? It exists as the ultimate tripper like loose shoelaces.

On Travels 10/22/2023 04:53 AM

Freedom is the elusive and costly destination. An elusive prey.

On Crookedness 10/23/2023 04:08 PM

Sometimes life streams so crooked the mobile phone betrays. Big Tech demons live well. Soul takers, they are.

The House 10/2/2023 04:30 PM

The house is talkin' to me with creaks, bumps, and taps. "House, I don't like it any more than you do! It's called aging and wearing down." The downward ka-ching sounds rogue builders and traders crave and prey upon. No prayers made in such a rescue. On further introspection, insects, birds, and squirrels; rats, mice, and spiders wish for a home of their own. Mine. I'm just another tenant.

Every Change 10/23/2023 04:39 PM

The seasons heap a bounty or flood upon the senses biological and fanciful Bring reminders of the chaos in changes and the specific invaders chomping a way into the feasting halls.

Little Crumbs 10/23/2023 05:17 PM

Have to hand it to philosophers. They hide no qualms regarding expressions of humanity as merely another invader upon the landscape of life forms.

On Politicians 10/23/2023 05:23 PM

Turn off the chaos spigot of politicians and the chaos will wither and die from lack of nourishment.

On Human Inanity 10/25/2023 02:44 PM

Are humans so lonely on Earth they relentlessly search for species or potential friends inhabiting other universe orbs? If we're lonely here on Earth, then another place is merely a place to remain lonely.

On Populace Control 10/25/2023 04:39 PM

Subjugation of the populace has been perfected by many earthbound governments. Perfect examples exist, akin to China, Russia, Iran, and the United States of America.

Banshee Curse (Story Idea) 10/26/2023 12:50 AM

Relatively unknown author finally granted a spot at a local bookstore to give away signed copies of his penned novels; a fan visits, attempts romantic overtures directed to the author; he is not responsive as he just went through a rough and tumble marriage and finalized the divorce; he starts to believe the ex-wife put the "fan" up to this stunt. The fan is so persistent he rebuffs her not gently, then as she walks away he whispers, "dream on". She stops but doesn't turn, in a manner that eerily disturbs the author. His stomach seems to have dropped out of his intestinal function as if recovering from spoiled food ingestion. He begins to pass out, lastly hearing a sound of the front bookstore entrance/exit jingle.

On Responsible Citizenship 10/26/2023 06:04 PM

The government must never forget who pays the bills.

On Age Adaptation 10/27/2023 08:57 PM

Getting a leg up, at any age, can become a challenge which increases at any time future.

On A Geneva Convention 10/27/2023 09:53 PM

There's nothing but cook book arbitrators telling us how not to roast a monster. A best seller for fools and their politician ilk of corruptocrats. The persecuted know much better how to prepare and display a peaceful civilization dinner.

On Mongrels of Leftist Genes 10/28/2023 11:34 AM

They who seek misery or death for those not them will never be happy nor satisfied. Beware. Be aware.

On Roaming 10/28/2023 12:08 PM

There's a song about roaming around the world. Interesting philosophy, but in all such thought processes, risks abound amidst wisdom rewards.

Of No Return 10/28/2023 01:41 PM

As humans, we tend to become bugged by a desire for a return to past places lived, visited, experienced in some means or matters. Just another temptation to make mental connections amidst the mind network.

No Exit 10/28/2023 01:43 PM

Get out! Get out! Begone from this brainbox!

On Syncing Sinking 10/28/2023 01:49 PM

Going up or going down arrives at a destination of near known unknown.

Caveat: changing or rearranging thoughts tempts a brink of destruction predictable but many times such a breach desires a hide behind a curtain or hide inside a closet.

<u>On Geometry</u> 10/28/2023 01:55 PM

Go figure.

<u>On Weary Mind Moments</u> 10/28/2023 01:57 PM

The last pack of smokes and the last can of brew casts a bleak shadow of mind overtures.

<u>On Perspective Zones</u> 10/28/2023 02:30 PM

Imperfection exists as a form of perfection. Completion exists as a form of incompletion.

<u>On Points</u> 10/28/2023 02:30 PM

There is a point to getting to the point. Even forever beacons a destination. Books, or the readings thereof, serve as examples. I've almost never read, word for word, a complete literary work. They display too much inactive time. Meals, however, portray a much different story. Every single crumb desires, requires, consumption.

<u>Bread</u> 10/28/2023 04:42 PM

"If a picture paints a thousand words then why can't I paint you?" First lyric line from the soft rock song "If," (1971) written by David Gates.

<u>Pickle Juice</u> 10/28/2023 04:44 PM

Tastes better than orange juice.

<u>On Love</u> 10/28/2023 05:16 PM

Who am I? What am I? Where am I? It doesn't matter. All that matters is you. Through grief and relief; through time and rhyme; through downs and crowns; win that moment together, and win life's race.

<u>On Life Span</u> 10/29/2023 12:36 PM

Life begins at an involuntary stage of acceptance, then slowly progresses into the voluntary state of rejection.

<u>Songs That Remind Me of Former Lovers</u> 10/29/2023 12:55 PM

Night Moves, by Bob Seger

Super Freak, by Rick James

Two Out of Three Ain't Bad, by Meat Loaf

Same Old Lang Syne, by Dan Fogelberg

September, by Earth, Wind, & Fire

<u>Nothin' Special</u> 10/29/2023 01:23 PM

The universe is a narcissistic gas lighter.

<u>Plans</u> 10/29/2023 06:03 PM

Escape from the past. Live in the present. Plan for the future.

<u>Keep on Truckin'</u> 10/29/2023 06:06 PM

One foot in front of the other at a one day at a time pace. Sometimes, two steps back required to recalculate distances.

<u>Visions</u> 10/29/2023 10:55 PM

Humans smiling is a beauty quality bestowed upon no other mammals. Such a rare gift it is. Still, not often enough used as expression.

<u>Time Depreciations</u> 10/30/2023 or 2032? 12:03 AM

One day can be made the difference, but many of darks moons must rise and fall first.

<u>Tom(b) Foolery</u> 10/30/2023 08:53 PM

What's the difference between a fool and an idiot? A fool knows who is an idiot.

<u>On Noise</u> 10/31/2023 03:03 AM

Could be a book title about sounds such as voices creaking in the night of weather related/climate changes which affect both objects, creatures, and humans. Maybe explore in the details a competition of life amidst itself, i.e. in the single body versus other life forms. Future writings may involve more so these earthly biology interactions, and less so the actions of living human/humanoid interactions. Biology is the engine of the story plot. The mind can only focus on one or a few things at once which causes a drowning out or distraction of attention while inhabiting greater in scope surroundings. A shopping mall versus a church chapel.

<u>On Music</u> 10/31/2023 03:14 AM

The poetry in and of music almost never disappoints.

<u>Walls</u> 10/31/2023 03:16 AM

The movements inside walls, particularly at night, stirs eerie weary mind adventures.

<u>Bedding Down Frustrations</u> 10/31/2023 03:21 AM

The placement of the human body upon the bed matters. Is reminiscent of a dog turning around in a circle.

<u>On Relaxation</u> 10/31/2023 03:36 AM

What is relaxation? Just kidding. Practically begging the mind and body to relax. I used to be able to do this method, focusing thoughts, trying to get in touch with the muscle groups of the legs and lower body and changing focus gradually up to my shoulders, neck, and head, but aging seems to have made the concentrations aspect of the endeavor more of a challenge.

<u>Speed Falls</u> 11/02/2023 07:17 PM

In this current human age when stupidity evolves at the speed of light, perhaps wisdoms will do the same.

<u>On Selling Ideas</u> 11/02/2023 07:20 PM

Prostitution has humorously been claimed to be the oldest profession, but in the process of selling sexual wares as temptations, one finds marketing towards sales as the horse pulling the cart of delights and other miseries.

<u>Middle Ages Thought</u> 11/02/2023 07:25 PM

Freedom isn't an either-or proposition. Half-wit barbarous cultures only think such. Who were their teachers?

<u>Love's Value</u> 11/04/2023 01:40 PM

Love is worth more than money. Used to think such anyway. Love is used as subterfuge to lie, cheat, and steal, consistently.

<u>On Pharmacy</u> 11/05/2023 08:20 AM

If a pharmacist exists who might develop an instant happiness drug, then the world could chemically become a much happier and friendly place at business, workplace, government, social and family gatherings. All kinds of contraindications possible. Could also lead to nightmares, paranoia, suicidal thoughts. The sidewalks, streets, and alleys could be lined with incredibly happy addicted humans/humanoids. Upon further consideration, an efficient means to control the populace, or make them oblivious to the obvious destruction the elites would unleash upon the happy powerless enabled. Much evidence exists in the cities of the near silent groans and moans of such current conditions.

<u>Broken On Repeat</u> 11/05/2023 10:26 AM

I did it all for you and you broke it all. I did it all for you again and you broke it all again. I did it all for you once more again and you broke it all once more again. So, I left it all broken.

<u>Peace Pieces</u> 11/05/2023 10:31 AM

You never really have it all worked out.

<u>Now</u> 11/07/2023 10:31 AM

Here it is, another day, progressing as nature designed, accompanied by numerous human modifications; all entities marching along, above ground in the air and upon the landscapes, and below in the rivers and seas. All timed subject to the sun's mercies intended.

<u>Tyranny's Evolution</u> 11/08/2023 02:29 PM

When the government becomes too powerful in a society once organized as a republic, it is because the chains clipped to the general public citizens were forged in taxation fires. Look out your window. All that you see has been taxed. Look in your dwelling cabinets and closets. Almost all has been taxed.

Taxation exists as an assault upon all that is good about a citizen's freedoms. Easiest means to erode those freedoms is to tax them from birth to death. The list of taxed goods and property rivals the number of stars in the heavens.

<u>Universal Construction</u> 11/09/2023 03:01 PM

During construction of the universe, I sometimes wonder if it included a basement, and if so, is it a finished or unfinished basement.

<u>Nature's Rule</u> 11/10/2023 10:08 PM

Nature seems to abhor the carpenter's level tool as many sidewalks, over time, tilt and crack, making a comfortable walk a human's nightmare of face plant varieties.

<u>On Laws</u> 11/10/2023 10:13 AM

Rule of law exists as an interpretative dance of farcical calculations and miasmas.

<u>On Food Bells</u> 11/10/2023 10:57 PM

There are many reasons to eat or not to eat. A daily struggle lives.

<u>Thoughts Random</u> 11/11/2023 04:42 PM

Crumb-less food. Just an idea.

<u>On Cursing</u> 11/11/2023 09:13 PM

What in the fracking furk! I feel so much better now.

<u>On Senses</u> 11/13/2023 08:48 AM

The senses work as an illuminator usable during offensive and defensive human needs. For instance, odor and a sniff thereof acts as a self-defense mechanism.

<u>On Movement</u> 11/13/2023 08:57 AM

Time. Emit.

<u>On Slavery</u> 11/14/2023 12:15 PM

Why hasn't it occurred to the citizenry that governments use the economy like a terroristic bioweapon?

<u>On Seeds</u> 11/14/2023 03:14 PM

The seeds of imagination are a virulent bunch.

<u>Philosophy</u> 11/15/2023 09:57 PM

Religions seem more to my mind as philosophies geared towards somewhat noble ideals put into daily practice, and not as quintessential cultural mandates.

<u>Appreciation</u> 11/15/2023 10:29 PM

One day these harried times will diminish in frequency, and when they do, the upside is an appreciation for a willingness to make your own owned dreams come true.

<u>Work Mantra March</u> 11/15/2023 11:31 PM

A long and windy trudge. The Management Class of just about any company qualifies as certifiably insane. For instance, in some jobs, managers insisted on following the rules in the printed employee manual. Some of the manuals read like glorified Study Guide pamphlets high school and college students could purchase at any bookstore. The manuals served as somewhat a cheat sheet outline. English Majors sometimes used them when their part-time economic support jobs cut into study time, so the quick study guides helped a bit.

Anyway, some workplaces, especially insurance companies, had more than 3,000 pages divided into sub-group categories like an Encyclopedia. Employees were expected to read and consult the manuals as needed. The manual for one place numbered in mostly unreadable pages longer than a traditional Bible. How to determine a "need" was never explained.

Naturally, this circumstance allowed Management to downgrade an employee's performance rating for not learning the required materials. Catch-22 Anyone? Management patted themselves on the back for their bonuses while they castigated employees for not learning the necessary material.

Suddenly, Management must have been castigated, because they then promoted a "think outside the box" mantra, in other words it was okay to make mistakes (like them, which they never admitted), as means to discover the "mythical" best practices formula. The Einsteins in the non-management worker group would be rewarded with long-distance phone call freebie cards up to $25. None of us could afford to make long distance calls anyway, and we had long abandoned such a practice, so the cards went unused. The free phone cards made rather good coffee cup coasters.

Another offshoot of Management failure passing the burden onto the workforce involved an unfamiliar word to describe "castigation". The unfamiliar word was tossed around daily, not just by Management, but by public media outlets, college professors, politicians and the usual self-absorbed and self-proclaimed Masters of the Universe.

The unfamiliar word use became "unacceptable". It was used so often against workers they started to consider it as appropriate as "fuck". So, the word "unacceptable" meant to hurl a curse word. Eventually, we used it to curse Management during social hours. Crazy as fuck morphed into crazy as unacceptable.

So, the work rules evolved over forty plus years from "follow the rules" into "think outside the box" and finally into "unacceptable". True story. Vacuous is as vacuous does.

<u>Choices Made</u> 11/16/2023 01:06 PM

Votes for a politician known by actions and facts as corrupt means the voter is fine with corruption, and further, likely benefits from such vile circumstances.

<u>You Only Live Once</u> 11/16/2023 02:03 PM

Sometimes once is too much.

<u>On Temperatures, Temperaments</u> 11/16/2023 02:09 PM

Which is more unpredictable, the weather or human temperaments?

<u>On gods</u> 11/16/2023 07:18 PM

Gods work in mysterious ways doesn't cut it as the answer to any question. I wouldn't hire them to fix my car or provide maintenance to it.

On Classified Gov Docs 11/17/2023 01:10 PM

Presidents and their underlings shouldn't be permitted to mark documents as classified when the documents implicate them and underlings in criminal or immoral activity.

On Civilization 11/18/2023 10:06 AM

In many civilizations, the citizens have needed to defend themselves against corrupt and murderous rulers. Nothing has changed. The reasons ring obvious.

To Candace 11/18/2023 10:52 AM

No more a perfect human can one be than the type who walks softly yet is willing to sting like a bee.

Goal Scores 11/19/2023 10:53 AM

It's only impossible if you don't try.

Travails 11/19/2023 11:27 AM

One's soul can become lost while expending blood, sweat, and tears to the demands of a cause wary, but may be recaptured amidst the drum beats of virtuous deeds weary.

On Nags 11/19/2023 12:28 PM

No matter how much trying is involved, the crumbs won't die.

<u>Urges and Purges</u> 11/19/2023 01:03 PM

Open this, open that. Love flies around like a fussy gnat.

<u>On Imagination Imaging</u> 11/21/2023 08:54 PM

Loopy cute. Many faces appear in the mind.

<u>Self Defense Economics</u> 11/23/2023 09:29AM

It occurs to me, as I'm sure it does to corrupt politicians who likely profit from criminal activities perpetrated against citizens, that a significant taxpayer cost savings would accrue if criminals in the acts of crime commission are shot dead on site. Self-defense provides for a deadly economic efficiency. Politicians abhor efficiency. They might be made to become unnecessary.

<u>On Politician Schemes</u> 11/23/2023 09:41 AM

Government efficiency can be defined as enacting laws which mandate a solution model designed to create more problems.

<u>On College Miseducation</u> 11/23/2023 07:01 PM

College professors, by and large, teach propaganda to muddy student minds. When that mud hardens into dirt, then the students become stuck in it, and the "it" foments cultural doom. Free yourself from such an inglorious miasmatic filth. Risk the retribution and insult from other students who have fallen as prey programmed not to think. Forcibly taught to primarily obey, or else, is not teaching. It is tyranny.

<u>On Toddler World and Works</u> 11/24/2023 01:20 PM

As a very young child I obsessed over making things, taking objects and the trying to connect them together or join them as means to gain greater importance and utility. My favorites were building blocks. They came in varied shapes and sizes like squares, triangles, X's, O's, L's. Also played with Army figures in varied plastic soldier ranks and poses, all a dark green in color, would become incorporated into and around my structure builds. I sometimes wondered about my almost obsessive need for such time usage. Taking toys and turning them into a vision my mind produced helped to escape the chaos and constraints of the real world, and allowed my toddler vision to seek out another place.

On 12 Worded Blessings 11/24/2023 03:53 PM

May you reside amidst the most serene human and other creature harmonies.

On Human Pigs 11/25/2023 02:27 AM

Politicians who hang around too long in their elected positions, either truthfully or under false pretenses, can accurately be characterized as pigs for power.

On Porcupines 11/25/2022 02:50 AM

Seems to me, given a porcupine's defense mechanism of extending the hairs on their bodies into sharpened skin piercers, then a human porcupine might classify as superhero.

Mannequins 11/26/2023 10:26 AM

Could it be that time travels and all things, humans, creatures, objects, weathers, seas, remain stationary?

On Age 11/26/2023 10:31 AM

At some point, age progression is nothing but rotting.

On a Happy Moment 11/26/2023 10:57 AM

When an old friend comes around to see you, and each of you gets to say "Hi", and no needs are discussed, just only deeds done.

On Knowing Others 11/26/2023 11:48 PM

The greatest farce of all in human/humanoid history is we think we know each other. We don't. The thought is merely another warm blanket comfort fictitious.

Silly Putty 11/27/2023 02:18 PM

Time is a relevant and relative elastic, much like a disease or virus.

More Silly Putty 11/27/2023 02:41 PM

If time was treated much like doctors treat a disease, then maybe we could cure ourselves of it.

On Baking 11/27/2023 04:35 PM

The proper way to bake another's opinion is to first marinade it in a bowl of perspective.

Sounded Rounded Scales 11/29/2023 04:14 PM

Humans seem to emit a musical scale of sound, to my ears, blaring out as clarinet, saxophone, and trombone. Physical demonstrations and emotional essences notwithstanding.

On Abortions 11/30/2023 05:13 PM

First we abort our children and lose intelligence, then we abort our words and lose our sentience.

Marmalade (Story Idea) 12/01/2023 02:45 AM

A food, poisoned. A human/humanoid name. First or last? Ethnic or cultural connections? What's the story about? Theme: there exists spirits around us hovering, not sure from which world, or is it a dimension, but the MC (main character) knows now (how discovered?) they put ideas and inspirations into our heads that itch and scratch our minds into possible actions, possible choices.

Time Pings 12/01/2023 04:25 AM

Time moved slow as moments swerved fast in barely enough moments to capture the past.

On Memories 12/01/2023 04:33 AM

Can one remember the days of the energetic past, or evenings when the dinner bell rang in the mind's blast?

<u>On Knocks</u> 12/01/2023 04:35 AM

Who is there at the door's knock? Someone, maybe her?

<u>On mind gremlins</u> 12/01/2023 04:39 AM

The gremlins in my mind clammer for words to write in hopes a dance or prance feverish might ignite.

<u>On Space</u> 12/01/2023 03:33 PM

There is much more comfort in the smallness of living space.

<u>Jesus of Nazareth</u> 12/01/2023 10:44 PM

Jesus Christ has become so popular his very name has been used as a curse. Be wary of 3 syllabled names?

<u>On Obvious Challenges</u> 12/02/2023 12:34 AM

Confront your weaknesses and slay them or continue running circles around yourself until neglect of purpose squeezes you into an inescapable and tiny dot on the page of life.

On Human Creatures 12/02/2023 01:49 PM

Born a human is both a beautiful and horrible life experience. The mind is a cruel master to the slave body.

On the Life Train 12/02/2023 02:22 PM

There is no love without pain. No beauty without struggle. No joy without sorrow. No success without failure. No solemnity without raucous enmity.

On Seconds and Follicles 12/02/2023 09:17 PM

Time and beauty are both fleeting and fleeing at a constant rate.

On Living Effectively by Means 12/04/2023 11:09 AM

If many of these rich people out there want to live like monks, they should have at it. Meanwhile, us commoners will continue to seek out available, resilient, and cost-effective methods to make and keep us comfortable and fed.

Dread Bork (Story Idea) 12/04/2023 11:19 AM

Title: Things You Never Do for Me

A mythical creature, Dread Bork, exhibits a depressive personality, but becomes stronger when stressed into anger.

On Politics in the "Free" World 12/04/2023 11:28 AM

We trust and elect politicians believed to be potential stewards of the republic, yet generally or regularly they demonstrate our trust is misplaced.

On Weather 12/05/2023 10:43 PM

We say sunny, as in "it's sunny out", but we don't say moony. Not sure why.

On Management 12/06/2023 09/27 AM

Managers work as if they are not required to work, then blame their employees for every failure. Hey, buttheads.

Work.

On Ambiguous Laws 12/06/2023 10:43 PM

In the 21st century it seems every government has a law miscellaneous and unwritten, at times, but often written which states something like "any speech or activity engaged in which corresponds to the previously delineated words or actions upon another". The word "corresponds" becomes a trap door sprung by corrupt governments and their "miscellaneous" affiliated entities.

<u>Essence Man (Story Idea)</u> 12/07/2023 11:49 PM

Average height, weight, somewhat muscular, dark hair, hazel eyes, imbued by an essence supernatural which he can use to overtake and control the senses, sensations, and sensibilities of all living things, but he must be careful how and when he wields such influence strength, for it can make or change his world both great and small.

<u>On Life Socialization</u> 12/08/2023 12:04 AM

Life isn't a room where the most easily triggered human rules the roost.

<u>On Switches</u> 12/09/2023 12:21 PM

(I know what you were thinking there. The sounds were evident.)

Wouldn't we live longer lives if we achieved an ability to shut down to minimum the energy system of the body; an ability to shut down blood flow, so body and mind could achieve Zen-type rest.

On Beauty's Siren Song 12/09/2023 01:01 PM

My attraction to her was so strong that I became afraid of it. Her hair is golden. Her eyes are blue. Her aroma is sweet. Her voice was angelic. Each quality reached out to me as temptation so magnetic I risked drowning in her existence whirlpool.

On Doctor's Offices 12/11/2023 11:03 AM

Sitting in the doctor's office waiting for my appointment is a good time to see new faces, hear new names, observe facial expressions, voice tones, discover varied aromas, sounds of sneezing or wheezing human or otherwise. The mechanisms and layouts of the buildings speak, too.

On Spaces 12/11/2023 11:09 AM

A table devoid of surface ornaments is a lonely place.

On Reliability 12/11/2023 11:23 AM

I once knew a three-legged dog was more dependable than my mobile phone.

<u>On Medical Evals</u> 12/12/2023 10:10 AM

Day two post fainting spells, the cause a mystery, lurks still like eye contact amongst Waiting Room patients.

"Figure It Out Yourself"

<u>On Governments</u> 12/15/2023 10:24 AM

Governments are wolves. Hungry wolves, voracious in appetite. Government citizens and illegals are sheep, readied for the slaughter. No buts about it.

<u>On California</u> 12/15/2023 10:26 AM

The government has provided citizens many reasons to commit crimes.

<u>On New York</u> 12/15/2023 10:28 AM

See above, <u>On California</u>.

<u>On Baltimore</u> 12/15/2023 10:29 AM

The mayor is on permanent lunch break.

On humans 12/15/2023 10:51 AM

Humans have always been stone throwers. The Aussies know better. See the boomerangs. Throw it and it comes back to hit the thrower.

On Cancel Culture 12/15/2023 11:15 AM

In medieval times there existed government hired executioners who took away the physical existence of the accused. In woke times there exists self-designated executioners who take away the social and monetary existence of the accused.

On humanoids 12/15/2023 12:03 PM

All humanoid species exist exactly as at first eggs, then as flesh sacks, and eventually internal bones, organs, and other life sustaining accoutrements. Age groups, as it were. On every habitable orb, in every galaxy.

On Construction Wizardry 12/15/2023 01:50 PM

Taking a back yard smoke in the city. Quite amazing how construction and electricity workers can put together telephone and electrical poles with wires attached, insulators routing the currents needed to power homes, schools, businesses like taverns and grocery stores and tire stores and miscellaneous handy needs and wants shops and more. The insulators shine like works of art.

Truth Glare 12/16/2023 09:02 AM

Untidy truths tend to tidy up the mind's view much like a sunglasses effect.

On The Judgment Effect 12/16/2023 09:12 AM

Perspective often forms a precedent for judgment, truth be damned. A somewhat ultimate human trait and sometimes fault of devastating consequences.

Satan's Stroller (Story Idea) 12/16/2023 12:57 PM

An investigative reporter, hired by a Christian Weekly magazine, sets out to find Satan's stroller. Whether one ever existed depended on the religious belief of the person interviewed for the story.

Research: Beliefs of and myths of ancient civilizations. A seeming endless journey ending after reporter leaves his last investigative destination. A stroller surrounded by a dazzling orange glow sits still in a dark alley nearby, then starts rolling on its own. Religions: Christian,

Catholic, Islam, Hindu, Daoism, Satanism, Paganism, and more.

<u>Attack of the Killer Pillows (Story Idea)</u>
12/17/2023 01:16 PM

Pillows attack!

An adult female asleep, about to be smothered by a house burglar when the burglar's attempt is stalled by a counterattack of the pillow. The pillow defended the woman, much like a dog's defensive mechanisms operate. Police investigate.

Research: pillow types. Pillow ingredients (cursed materials?) How and where pillows are made. Product distribution.

<u>On The Rogue Winds</u> 12/18/2023 04:27 PM

Sometimes the wind sounds out like schoolyard children running around and about the midday playgrounds.

<u>On The Rogue Skies</u> 12/18/2023 05:31 PM

The Sun, so shy, allows only a sleepy glance of the eye. The Moon, a seductress, reveals bit by bit a peek long and deep as the show continues for a month in time steep.

On Politics 12/18/2023 07:11 PM

Freedom of speech, if you can afford it.

On Error 12/22/2023 07:50 AM

Some mistakes you never stop paying for.

Warning: Don't read out loud this blurb when friends, family, and pets are within earshot.

On Candles 12/22/2023 08:36 AM

There is no light without the candle.

On Weakness 12/22/2023 10:49 AM

Humans often attempt to make themselves feel better by finding faults in others.

Time Dance 12/22/2023 11:00 PM

Sometimes interesting when thinking of the present, the past intrudes and asks, "may I have this dance?".

On Ass Wobble 12/24/2023 03:18 PM

Politicians are so deviously sweet while they shit tootsie rolls.

On Trusts (Not Estates) 12/25/2023 11:40 AM

Trust is that bird twitch readied to flee at the slightest hint of non-avian contact.

On Warring Societal Factions 12/27/2023 11:38 AM

Write to enlighten, and not to instigate fightin'.

On Bias 12/27/2023 01:01 PM

Every creature is afflicted by a brain bias of survival necessity. The brain calculates the reasoning process on the road to a final conclusion. A cat walks by a mirror and sometimes sees the reflection as a threat. Incorrect conclusions can warp creature perspectives leading to activities dangerous. The cat may jump towards and into the mirror, claws drawn, readied to strike further. Substitute the word "human" for "cat" and further revelations shout back into the cranium pot, then a stir poisonous, and a society stew begins to brew unholy.

On Starting Lines 12/28/2023 10:33 PM

In the beginning. Ominous words. What comes forth stings.

<u>On Creature Movements</u> 12/28/2023 12:26 PM

Enjoy the movements of creatures great and small. An intriguing and refreshing experience awaits, even amongst human folly.

<u>On Necessary Adjustments</u> 12/29/2023 07:02 AM

When younger, life was all about speeding up. Now much older, it is all about slow…down, slow…down, slow…down.

"Three...two…one…Happy Know Year!"

<u>Creep Goes The Night</u> 01/01/2024 04:08 PM

Possible story title and theme. Research to determine if title used previously.

<u>On Memory Ability / Disability</u> 01/02/2024 10:40 AM

Short term memory loss. Is it a curse or a blessing? Depends on the situation. The situation doesn't change unless choices are made. Some benign, some critical. The memory of the situation then determines storability time. Notepads act like therapy for such circumstances. Each page asks "send to trash can", or "store it".

On Everyday Living 01/02/2023 11:33 AM

Every day is a load of bullshit navigation. Just have to learn a way to navigate through, over, or around it. See the cities.

On Coinage 01/02/2024 02:53 PM

The government coins metals. The author coins words.

On Eating Habits 01/02/2024 05:15 PM

Some eat crumbs, whether paid for them or not.

On Ransacking a Dead Man 01/03/2024 11:20 AM

Need anything else beaded? Abominable.

On Life Existence Scales 01/03/2024 12:01 PM

Not trying to become a hero. Just trying to avoid becoming a zero.

On Rogue Thoughts 01/04/2024 10:03 AM

Stupid thoughts enter a human's head all the time. Fortunately, they don't regularly act on them.

On Mind Resparking 01/05/2024 07:46 AM

A taste of humble pie. Don't give a rat's ass. Sometimes such thoughts or statements jigger the mind into an appropriate phase.

On House Sounds 01/05/2024 07:48 AM

Houses make noises, randomly. Worries spark in the mind. Imagination, too, sparks.

On The Eve of Evening 01/06/2024 11:34 PM

In the twilight a world looks different. The sun day's sheen wanes. Time then ticks for the night wolf's bane. All measures are brought to bear as evening balances daytime despair. As loss encroaches upon gains of the day, another day spent is the toll to pay. Good fortune awaits at dawn's booth payment to play. Damn. There's always something else in need of an imprint.

On Living Life 01/09/2024 12:01 PM

Love is a song sung blue.

On Crows 01/12/2024 11:37 AM

Can you hear the crows marching?

On 21st Century Life 01/12/2024 12:55 PM

We now live in a world where Big Tech moguls obtain data about our lives, then determine what we want and need even before we know it. A most perfect way, utility, to at last imprison us en masse. Our wants and needs have been bought and sold to the highest market bidders.

On Species Manipulation 01/12/2024 01:01 PM

A world of need and greed. A circus time of want and taunt.

On The Oculus 01/14/2024 02:26 PM

How to see as a seer using the fingers and thumb? Can see near present future? Third eye soothsayer or Ouija Board and interested minds touching upon the pointer?

On Shift in Clarity 01/16/2024 09:26 AM

I heard a news media reporter say "shift in clarity" after a factual statement presented to her regarding border security, and all that came to mind for me about her new clarity perspective was that she decided to pull her head out of her ass about the matter.

On Governments Three P's 01/17/2024 10:13 AM

In this century the primary purposes of government officials have evolved into overt selective prosecution and persecution, adding further, punitive links to citizen slavery chains.

On Story Inspiration 01/20/2024 02:13 PM

An author's inspiration begins like a dream. A noise, a sound, a moving all around as vague images husked from that single ignition kernel ascend into a reveal.

On evolution's path 01/20/2024 10:07 PM

Tardigrades and springtails, wow.

On Human Oder 01/21/2024 01:12 PM

If humans smelled like crisp wafers in milk chocolate then the earth's population would become much larger in size.

On Gnats 01/21/2024 06:54 PM

In recent years (2,500 or so) humans have displayed the characteristics of gnats, swarming in large groups to varied mostly city-sized locales.

On Distant Memories 01/22/2024 03:49 AM

One of the first sentient thoughts of my childhood years popped into the head like a slap: "who are these creatures hovering around me?" They seemed so weird. Then, one day, I discovered a mirror, and realized I was one of "them". Mommy stopped me from head-butting it. Took a while to get used to this realization.

On Social Groupings 01/22/2024 04:00 AM

Let all the narcissists out narcissist each other. Let all the passive aggressive aggressively out passive each other. Let all the extroverts out shout each other. Let all the introverts out silence each other. These are the groups who need segregation by group. Segregation is the fools game of intellectual safety.

On Political Language 01/22/2024 10:41 AM

All the political parties have propagandist media which vape the language they utter. They can stuff it where the sun doesn't shine. They are worthless puke humans hired to depress the minds of the populace. Evil.

<u>On Corrupt Politics Cities</u> 01/22/2024 10:49 AM

A lot of these cities aren't populated by a singular, legal generational political group but instead are infested by them. Some parts of every such politicized city evoke the looks and sounds of a war zone.

<u>AI Wars</u> 01/22/2024 11:57 AM

Food products slowly turn humans into humanoid AI bots. This human story is a familiar one of porky and corrupt growth, but is slowly becoming filtered into a permanent and unreversible condition aided by rich elites who ride the high tide and know they will be long gone before complete destruction of the human culture arrives. The government is funded unwittingly by human citizens as a means to stoke the totalitarian inclinations of the political rulers. "This one, be wary of it." How they talk about citizens they despise; the citizens who refuse to conform. We've all heard the endearing voices of politicians. The sweeter the sound, the sourer the intent.

<u>On Moving On</u> 01/22/2024 12:56 PM

Move on. A broken heart never mends.

On Memory Jolts 01/22/2024 01:01 PM

Fevered ire, a flat tire, such moments seek to be rendered from memories' iron fire.

On Non Sequiturs 01/22/2024 01:50 PM

Nonsense is the sense of none.

On Losing 01/23/2024 09:36 AM

When you've got nothing to lose you've got nothing to lose.

On Last Moments' Thoughts 01/25/2024 01:59 PM

Your momma loves you. Your daddy loves you. Your daughters love you. Your sons love you. Your brothers love you. Your sisters love you. Your husband loves you. Your wife loves you. And I love you.

On Fertility 01/27/2024 02:49 AM

A fallow perspective propagates a fallow mind.

On Circumstance Evolution 01/28/2024 12:03 PM

We are all products or our own circumstances. We are all circumstances of our own products.

<u>On Relevance</u> 01/28/2024 12:15 PM

Each of us exists as a focus point of societal interaction and intervention.

<u>On Miserations Onward</u> 01/28/2024 01:44 PM

Eat up their death cakes, served to you courtesy of the local government corruptocrats. Your misery sustains their power and wealth.

<u>On Growing Ghouls and Goals</u> 01/28/2024 01:57 PM

Growing up often means confronting and slaying our inherited mind demons in order to pass towards a greater, more prescient existence sentience.

<u>On "Am I?"</u> 01/28/2024 01:59 PM

A single fiber of hair is proof of existence.

<u>On The Universe Knowledge</u> 01/28/2014 02:04 PM

Face it. All that has been written and read serves as a map, punched full of holes, to enlighten the who, what, when, where, why, and how. Any single text amalgamation of all human knowledge still sits as a dust speck in this universe's library. (yes, a dated thought from the past snuck into this narrative)

<u>On "Something In The Trees"</u> 01/28/2024 02:13 PM

A personal note to myself: see previous story outlines for book titles, three novels, numerous short stories. Sometimes I'm working on multiple ideas at once. Seems the ideas, etcetera, come from long and deep views into the trees.

<u>On Dialectical Dialect</u> 01/30/2024 10:05 AM

Kind a maybe.

<u>On Shut Up Theory</u> 01/30/2024 01:04 PM

We need a National Politician Ball Gag Day, or perhaps a week, or better yet, a month. All elected political party members in any capacity are required to properly wear ball gags when working.

<u>On The One</u> 01/31/2024 07:22 AM

There is no tool, no book, no idea that is the one key to any thing or everything.

On Human Relationship Snores 02/01/2024 12:12 AM

To not become able to perceive, or an inability to precisely perceive the mind machinations of another human, particularly if facial expressions serve as a masking agent, or conversely, emit an expression like a clown face carnival abstraction, is the scariest moment in existence. Relations and relationships are based on, and grounded upon a hope of truthful expressions, but such truth no x-ray or surgical scalpel can determine of any significance.

On Socializing Fantasies 02/02/2024 01:58 PM

The good think about socializing is an opportunity to observe the human race. The bad think about socializing is an opportunity to witness all of the vile and foul moments of the human race. Still, such observations enrich the mind buckets of the fantasy writers.

On Waiting 02/04/2024 05:04 AM

Many hours in a lifetime people stand in front of a coffee machine or microwave oven, waiting. Add EV charging stations to the list.

Vague Observations Requiring Reader Contemplations

<u>On Banter</u> 02/04/2024 05:43 AM

Idiots in my head banter endlessly. Reach conclusions unholy. Seek pleasures amidst chaos.

<u>On Warmth Manners</u> 02/04/2024 05:55 AM

A pen tip absent a top marks as a human head minus a cap.

<u>On Answers</u> 02/04/2024 06:02 AM

Solutions don't find themselves. A significant search expedition must be mounted.

<u>On Opportunity Potential</u> 02/04/2024 06:15 AM

A birth creates an opportunity comprised of part fortune and part effort.

<u>On Thinking versus Speaking</u> 02/04/2024 08:08 AM

Sometimes ya just gotta' keep the mouth shut even though the brain keeps on talkin'.

<u>On Multiculturalism Studies</u> 02/04/2024 08:13 AM

People who hate themselves teaching other people how to hate themselves, and such a curriculum financed by witless nincompoops and corruptocrats. The positive efforts and effects somehow were drowned in advance like an unwanted puppy.

<u>On New Yorkers</u> 02/08/2024 08:57 AM

You can take the human out of the New Yorker, but you can't take the New Yorker out of the human.

<u>On Artistic Results</u> 02/08/2024 09:36 AM

Deceptions can exist as brutal once exposed, but some admiration is due towards beautiful crafting involved in the work.

<u>On Effort</u> 02/08/2024 09:33 AM

No matter how much and long we try, an actual conception of the universe can never be achieved, no matter how many humans attempt such absolute understanding. It can only be observed from the inside of the universe house.

<u>On Understanding</u> 02/08/2024 09:44 AM

A work in progress it is, once started, never finished either of intent or purpose, whether separated or intertwined.

On Layers 02/08/2024 09:47 AM

Life existence starts as layer one amidst many layers sequentially infinite.

On Incorporations 02/08/2024 09:52 AM

Understandings generally incorporate misunderstandings.

On Fixing Things 02/08/2024 10:03 AM

I'm at that age of "tired of fixing things". I permit the dust and the invisible beings therein to grow and flourish, yet still I understand they will extend no mercy when it is my time to pass.

On Yarn Balls 02/08/2024 10:13 AM

Animal, vegetable, mineral are scientific designations. Humans display a twisted yarn ball of biological threads.

On a Deed's Purpose 02/08/2024 11:18 AM

A misdeed sometimes serves a purpose beneficial, just as a beneficial deed serves a misdeed of purpose. Why must many life experiences reside inside a mask of mysterious and ambulatory results?

<u>On Crazy Evolution</u> 02/09/2024 11:47 AM

We grew up in a world when crazy was not normal, but in today's world crazy is normal, and those not accepted into the new age normal are persecuted as the crazy.

<u>On Happiness</u> 02/09/2024 09:39 PM

There are plenty of reasons to be angry, but not enough reasons to be unhappy. In many ways, unhappiness is a choice.

<u>On Odds and Evens</u> 02/09/2024 09:44 PM

What is at odds and what is at evens depends upon a devil's mix of circumstances.

<u>On Totalitarian Monsters</u> 02/13/2024 07:27 AM

Our alleged voted-into-office politicians repeatedly impose taxes, licensing fees, draconian laws upon us. Too many people enjoy, ignore, or submit to such enforced slavery.

On Totalitarian Monsters More 02/13/2024 10:08 AM

Financially assaulted by taxations, fees; socially assaulted by major media, Big Tech; morally assaulted by social tech, religious cultism. It's a miracle humans still exist.

On USA Interpretive Mime 02/13/2024 11:57 AM

Ununited States of Argyle, silently speaking in waves of pain. We all now evoke an underwater perspective, grasping for breaths, in a place where tears have no name.

On Post Scripts 02/13/2024 01:15 PM

When your city is chock full of homeless, illegals, perpetrators of all manner of crimes rampant, crap filled and drug needles sidewalks, then the locale ought to be accurately named a shity, and not a city.

On Science Ideas 02/13/2024 09:38 PM

Synthetic lungs. Disease curing viruses, fungi, molds. Hyperbaric magnet/anti-magnet propulsion. Hyperbaric gravity/anti-gravity propulsion.

On <u>Illicit Persuasions</u> 02/14/2024 07:45 AM

Marketing Companies are nothing but parasitic mind control agents. Find the source, institute the cure.

On <u>Distances</u> 02/14/2024 10:03 AM

This whole entire world of moments many, rests and wrests, on and in, a game of inches.

On <u>Education Evolution</u> 02/15/2024 09:59 AM

The purpose of education once served as enlightenment. Now it has evolved to serve as an intentional pursuit to keep us living in a dark cave.

On <u>Understanding</u> 02/15/2024 10:06 AM

All you can see mentally tends to be all you can understand intellectually. Proper reading and interpretation can modify results.

On <u>Knowledge Acquisition</u> 02/16/2024 08:34 AM

If there's one thing I know it is I don't know enough.

On <u>Day's Adventure</u> 02/17/2024 12:23 PM

Every day has potential to be better, worse, or the same. Take what the day offers and deal with it.

<u>On Highway Robbers</u> 02/18/2024 01:28 PM

Mostly what we all get from big tech and media is "buy, buy, buy". Need to most often if not always instigate the mind to say "bye, bye, bye". It's your life and finances, not theirs.

<u>On Biolosophy</u> 02/18/2024 05:11 PM

Biology and Philosophy can exist in the same realm. To be alive on earth is to be dead anywhere not earth. The opposite condition is also likely valid. Speculation exists. Duplicates of ourselves could live amidst alternate realities in the universe. No "scientific" proof yet offered.

<u>On Loss</u> 02/22/2024 08:35 AM

When all is lost then much can be found. After all is found then much can be lost.

<u>On AI</u> 02/23/2024 06:29 AM

Just another of too many propaganda tools. Propagandists love to play this game. A general high for them.

On Persuasive Methods 02/23/2024 06:47 AM

We live in an era that may be accurately defined as "Propaganda Wars". Buy this, buy that. Think this, think that. Believe this, believe that. Good this, good that. Evil this, evil that. Love this, love that. Hate this, hate that. Do this, do that. Stop this, stop that.

On mind crashes 02/24/2024 11:49 AM

Learn how to phase down the mind. Too many memory haunts at once will tend to crash it. Solemn sentience is a learned skill.

On human togetherness 02/24/2024 12:04 PM

The greatest misjudgment of all human kind involves the creation of a mutual and beneficial relationship. Many of life's factors intercede in the process, almost as a communal sabotage effort. Zen studies might help in the method of "finding". Finding "what" remains mystery.

On personhood 02/25/2024 08:44 AM

In every person exists a world unto itself, and if that person is either fortunate or persistent then another world in another person may be shared willingly. Abide dangers.

<u>On Processed Thought Cheese</u> 02/29/2024 05:33 AM

The only humans who want time to pass by faster are whores and children. Unfortunately, that statement is not entirely true.

<u>On Creep Sentience</u> 02/29/2024 07:45 AM

The longer one lives in a city or town run by corruptocrats, the more finely it is realized many of the inhabitants exist as creepazoids.

<u>On Enlightenment Entrails</u> 02/29/2024 10:03 AM

Trekking along the road to enlightenment is a dangerous and nasty business. Dodge and parry deftly.

<u>Search for On The Knowledge</u> 03/09/2024 09:43 AM

I'm sure you're a fine human, but that's not what I'm looking for, hon.

<u>On Writing Life</u> 03/10/2024 10:33 AM

Enjoying the life of a writer. Waited my whole life for a prolonged segment of free time and an ability to enjoy it more. Practiced for decades. Squeezed time into folds of other jobs and tasks. And now it presents smallish and pleasant victories, scattered amidst and amongst larger tasks and tastes.

On Living Life 03/10/2024 10:47 AM

Living life, happily ever after. Living life happily, ever after. Big difference.

On Life Time Passes 03/10/2024 10:53 AM

Piss, wish, diss, miss(or add "ing" to each word eruption, if preferred) our way through life.

Just Dreaming 03/10/2024 10:57 AM

A masterpiece (or, expert pierce) of philosophic ruminations that require sentient participation from reader or listener minds (or mindsets multiple of the individual human/humanoid).

On Thinking Moments 03/10/2024 11:05 AM

When I contemplate writing of anything, I set my mind out to hearken and hail all thoughts and perspectives towards participation. Then, I become editor for which of these pills serve needs or heeds of the contemplation prescription.

On Plus One 03/10/2024 11:09 AM

Sometimes it is a rainstorm and thunder blitz of thoughts, painful in the capture; sometimes gentle nudges from a rogue thrown pinky ball; sometimes wasp stings long and agonizingly remembered. Words appear like a musician's physical iterations of thought.

On Eating a Sandwich 03/10/2024 11:15 AM

Life lives in the trying and not just in the living and dying.

On "they" Identity 03/11/2024 10:09 AM

Who's "they". In research, it has been determined "they" exist as marketing research spooks. "They" are the fantastical unseen.

On Stupid Repeats 03/12/2024 08:19 AM

Stupid actions decreed righteous by corrupt media remain stupid actions.

On Front Porch Earth Paradise 03/15/2024 10:49 AM

I've seen paradise in the eyes of the woman who would set my heart free. The subsequent mosquito bite sort of ruined the vision.

On Politicians 03/15/2024 12:11 PM

The one and only prevalent purpose of politicians is enslavement of the populace in mind, spirit, and soul..

On This Universe 03/15/2024 03:21 PM

There is no eternity, at least not in this universe. There are no gods all-powerful nor unstoppable. There are creatures and beings and microscopic elements capable of great destruction and great beneficence. Such is the way and manner of being. Usefulness exists as the highest endeavor honor. Still, it can become grotesquely abused.

On Marketers Marketing 03/18/2024 08:09 AM

Avidly trying to convince the public at large to buy a product or service they don't need for a "low, low price" or payment terms not affordable, and god forbid, the "fine" print in the sales contract. Only Satan himself "loves" the fine print.

On Wizards of Odds 03/20/2024 01:55 PM

Bastards, bitches, and gender pretenders, oh my.

<u>On Madness Scales</u> 03/20/2024 11:15 PM

The early 21st century will be remembered as a time when madness became fashionable and normals were considered unfashionable.

<u>On Life Tired</u> 03/21/2024 09:13 PM

Tired of thinking about life. Tired of remembering. Tired of reminiscing. Tired of missing. Tired of lost moments, opportunities wasted, dreams unbasted. Tired of being tired. Tired of plug in wired only to suffer disconnection. Pursuits no longer tempt. Temptations escape lament. Tired.

<u>On Criminal Culpability</u> 03/22/2024 09:09 AM

Crimes against one are crimes against all.

<u>On Loudmouth Gunkers</u> 03/23/2024 10:59 AM

He didn't know what he was doin'. She didn't know what she was sayin'. He just regurgitated the mind-bastard gibberish of them which taught him. Them scandalous purveyors of broken; pieced-together potable puzzle pieces. Them boobs.

Them faux whores. Them scandalous bores. Brie time!

<u>On Radio</u> 03/24/2024 09:57 AM

It is a morning of memory invasions, mostly good ones, courtesy of WBJC radio.

<u>On Time Passages</u> 03/24/2024 10:46 AM

What used to be and what is have not much changed. The poem remains the same.

<u>On Woke Equality</u> 03/24/2024 12:17 PM

One day some wacko socialist-marxist-totalitarian monster will propose baby abortions mandatory based on race, creed, and ethnic origin. PS: That one day already happened over 100 years ago.

<u>On Politics Chimeras</u> 03/24/2024 12:25 PM

The fix is in during every politician election cycle. You'd almost have to think citizens enjoy the agony, pain, and suffering, as opposed to reveling in economic success invisible. Such a mindset is easily and logically explained as financial gains massively accrue to the vote cheaters, so why would they morally abandon such a profitable racket.

On Future Human Qualities 03/24/2024 12:39 PM

In the future, only 3 personality human types will be lawfully tolerated: makers, takers, and fakers. Hybrids of such categories will virulently become hunted and eliminated but only after State sanction. Of course, most of the hunted will suffer the actions of unsanctioned entities.

On Traverses Societal 03/27/2024 11:36 AM

Please pardon me as I step across your railroad tracks.

On the Key Bridge Collapse 03/27/2024 12:41 PM

Ghosts of the Key Bridge Collapse tragedy will be safeguarding the newest bridge replacement span for a long, long time.

On One-Way Streets 03/27/2024 04:46 PM

There exists a Microwave to heat up food items. Why is there no Microwave to cool food items down? I suppose refrigerators work, but would they adversely affect the food quality of the current refrigerated products?

Do we really know, or are we properly advised exactly what ingredients and chemicals were used to produce this food? A distribution of diabolically constructed food could become a bioweapon. Perhaps, already has.

On Final Words 03/27/2024 05:11 PM

I propose a novel burial law or ritual. For those humans whose legacy left is mostly chaos, a curse of final gravesite words should be "May you rest in chaos".

No Longer Can Temptation Be Resisted

On Democrat Media 03/27/2024 11:37 PM

Shit slinging Democrat media. Nothing but shit slinging babies in diapers. Turd herders. Worthy of a South Park TV portrayal.

On Goodnights 03/28/2024 09:37 AM

Goodnight Average Avenue. Tomorrow's another day. Get some rest. Don't die yet. Sleep world awaits.

<u>On Starting (Ready, Set, Go)</u> 03/29/2024 08:29 PM

The small space between the lines of this theme tablet ushers forth a path to what is printed on these following pages . . . .

<u>On Idiots</u> 03/31/2024 10:03 AM

I met a person once who proclaimed that he was an idiot, and there were not enough idiots in the world. The person was howling, too, and virulently insisted there must be more idiots indoctrinated into the social construct of idiocy, and it must embody soul and mind. Understand?

<u>On Latest Gens</u> 03/31/2024 11:18 AM

Destroyers gently of all things they don't wish to understand.

<u>On Government Crimes</u> 04/03/2024 11:13 AM

When a government refuses to prosecute violent citizens, then only one possible conclusion remains: the government and criminals sleep in the same bedroom.

<u>On Universe Mysteries</u> 04/03/2024 02:10 PM

Most of this universe consists of a view dark, to our eye's and telescope and satellite abilities. Reflected shadows. What lays in these shadows? What is the purpose and point of these shadows? Are they random non-light places? Or do they intentionally exist as comfort or escape zones? Too, this universe emits audible sounds. A communication network not yet adequately defined. Perhaps dark matter in the universe reflects our Earth oceans.

<u>On Time's Legacy</u> 04/03/2024 03:38 PM

Time sweeps away all, from moments to generations. Time cares naught about anything except itself. Perhaps it is able only to care about itself. Perhaps there is too a time dustbin, accompanied by a thick handled sweeper used to lance or to disperse detritus. Time is cursed to live alone, forever.

<u>On Chaos Theory</u> 04/03/2024 05:02 PM

In this world there is the chaos you know, the chaos you'd like to know, and chaos lite. To each their own.

<u>On Thought Stabs</u> 04/07/2024 01:05 PM

No one likes everything and everything likes no one. That's just the way it is in this life.

<u>On Time Passages More</u> 4/07/2024 07:33 PM

Time gives and time takes, whether we are asleep or awake. Time has no brake. Time takes no break. Time runs deep. Able to take the long leap. Quite athletic, it is.

<u>On Story Lines</u> 04/08/2024 10:05 PM

"It's time, pretty face."

<u>On Pathology Bents</u> 04/09/2024 12:15 PM

Pathological liars rule over this world.

<u>On Stopwatches</u> 04/09/2024 12:50 PM

"It's never too late" means the time is finally ripe.

<u>On Physics</u> 04/09/2024 12:52 PM

Is zero an odd or even number? Math texts claim it to be even, but my imagination says otherwise.

On Media Ignorance 04/10/2024 01:45 PM

Are city governments corrupt beyond repair? Are city governments corrupt? Just a few questions the media press almost never makes time to pose. Here's a possible answer. City governments maintain power using a pathological belief: they have a moral right to power and must remain in power to fulfill the mission.

On Looking 04/10/2024 03:59 PM

If you're not thrilled with the view, then don't look out the window. Or look long and deep out the window and find what your mind is missing.

On Wokeness 04/11/2024 12:01 AM

I'm not at all certain regarding any benefits derived from a cultural evolution that embraces an emotional slavery path.

On Yin and Yang 04/11/2024 10:34 PM

The art of existence entails a war between mind and body, yet sometimes a truce must be called as survival is deemed necessary.

On Vehicle Gear Modes 04/12/2024 11:51 AM

Bitch, Jerkoff, Redneck, Democrat, Republican, Independent. For EV's, ghost mode.

<u>On Human Anomalies</u> 04/12/2024 01:06 PM

We exist in a world where truth has become an anomaly.

<u>Author/Writer/Journalist Bosh</u> 04/12/2024 11:33 PM

Reality ejaculations created as fantasies.

<u>On Humanity Head Banging</u> 04/14/2024 10:59 AM

All the men opt for chemical surgical castration and transformation into women, and all the women follow an opposite direction pursuit as well. At this point, educators, government, physicians, and scientists control the beginning of human extinction. Bonus: the climate paranoids celebrate, toking themselves into oblivion.

<u>On "Scientists Say"</u> 04/14/2024 11:27 AM

Scientists admit they are farting attention grabbers bent on puffing the ego pipe.

<u>On Story Ideas / Titles</u> 04/17/2024 (pre-dawn AM)

Pulling Away The Dust (a blind visionary seizes enlightenment by the balls, and later pays the price)

The Times I Defeated The Devil (gore fest, had to stop writing it. Not sharing it here.)

Mister Coincidence (able to create accidents to prevent crime. He's truly not sure how he is able to do it. Just thinking how to prevent a crime in progress works. Sometimes he can see the crime in his mind, sometimes he can see it live. Sounds in his mind or in his environment seem to stimulate his reaction.)

… movin' on …

<u>On Lost Memories</u> 04/17/2024 02:13 AM

Something to cry over, those lost memories. Sometimes snippets remain, but a strain to remember the whole frustrates like the puzzle of lost pieces. The mind fills in the blanks as best it can. Memories tend to hide in the senses, especially of sound, smell, and taste. Music, aroma, flavor.

Precious life moments reside in the senses storehouse.

<u>Wedding Toast</u> 04/17/2024 02:32 AM

May all of the best last forever and a day.

<u>On Love</u> 04/17/2024 11:01 PM

Too many thoughts of love and why. Makes me cry. Makes me cry. I don't know why. I don't know why.

<u>On Trying Times</u> 04/18/2024 12:03 PM

These are times when tested people want to rip the souls out of the politicians who are ripping them off.

<u>On Humankind and Nature</u> 04/19/2024 12:26 PM

Nature doesn't give a shit about the family of humankind.

<u>On Worms</u> 04/25/2024 01:26 PM

Chase the worm. End up in the wormhole.

<u>On Fear</u> 04/27/2024 10:43 AM

I see in everyone's eyes a tiredness, and fear, as if a message has gone out, the end is near.

On Time to Fear 04/27/2024 11:18 AM

It seemed the people knew to fear even though they couldn't see what was coming.

On City Fare 04/27/2024 12:07 PM

Democrat: commit any crimes you want.

Republican: follow the laws.

On April Fools 04/29/2024 10:13 AM

In a world of fake coins, fake dollars, fake intelligence, fake educators, and fake people, what could go wrong?

On Dollar Sign Prophets 04/29/2024 07:53 PM

Profiting from inefficiency seems to be all the rage in the 21st century.

On Evolution Quirks 04/30/2024 06:45 PM

Some of our younger generation politicians have millions of social media followers, and there's all that's needed to know about the direction of earth planet evolution.

On Educational Mind Bogs 04/30/2024 06:47 PM

Our children generally spend more time in a week with teacher units than with parental units. The results are predictable.

<u>On Biology</u> 05/01/2024 12:30 PM

Biology doesn't lie. It has no need to.

<u>On Time Heartless</u> 05/01/2024 01:57 PM

Time steals all. Time steels all. Until the bell tolls.

<u>On Story Telling</u> 05/01/2024 04:47 PM

When the ending comes, the beginning is long forgotten.

<u>On Big Tech Treachery</u> 05/03/2024 02:15 PM

Big Tech has absconded with the knowledge base ingredients, and now bakes it into ideas for sale much like a bakery creates cakes, buns, bagels, cookies, and candy treats. Has even baked political elections and outcomes. The elite human classes can generally enter and access much of such knowledge manufactured, but any one not them the elites fear, so they only sell bits and pieces at a time. Most humanity is treated like spoon fed infants.

<u>On</u> 05/04/2024 09:03 AM

Huh. We're all the same idiots. Makin' the same mistakes.

<u>On Baby Uni</u> 05/04/2024 11:06 AM

The universe doesn't understand itself any more than we do.

<u>On Mind States/Statuses</u> 05/06/2024 12:37 AM

During conscious day to day times my mind sometimes struggles to intentionally recall memories, but while sleeping my subconscious mind peppers with them. Not sure why, but rather convenient a circumstance when working on my latest book writing adventure.

<u>On gods</u> 05/06/2024 09:01 AM

Why do our gods treat us so badly? Religious rationalizations are not permitted.

<u>On Shadow Angles</u> 05/06/2024 01:23 PM

A shadow rests on a two dimensional plain but from varied perception angles it appears in three dimensions risen.

<u>On Open Doors</u> 05/06/2024 10:48 PM

When a door is opened for anyone, from that moment anything can and will happen, good or bad or in between.

On Alphabets and Meaning 05/06/2024 10:52 PM

AI = artificial intelligence = a computer reading an encyclopedia and other previously human written data from multiple perspectives.

UI = undocumented immigrants = a country reading an economics text and political treatise from multiple perspectives.

On gods 05/06/2024 11:57 AM

First thing to know about gods is they are liars, cheats, thieves, and murderers. Pretty much explains their progeny.

On Reality Race 05/08/2024 02:53 AM

In the race of reality, ambivalence crosses the finish line first by a nose.

On Investments 05/09/2024 12:08 PM

If the world is full of thieves , then eventually you'll find yourself investing in them.

On the World 05/09/2024 12:11 PM

Have you seen someone kick over an ant hill. Yeah, it's something like that.

<u>On Memories</u> 05/10/2024 05:47 PM

Some past moments act as a blessing and a curse, together.

<u>On College Experiences</u> 05/13/2024 10:31 PM

If you've attended college, after a few semesters, you come to realize some of the professors seem one step outside the looney bin on a smoke break.

<u>On Corruption Ratio</u> 05/17/2024 05:33 PM

At this point in history, the question isn't what is corrupt, but what isn't corrupt.

<u>On Human Dreams</u> 05/19/2024 04:36 AM

He started out as Captain Everything and finished up as Captain Nothing.

<u>On Looking Up Sometimes</u> 05/19/2024 08:47 AM

Not much thought is given to the sky except for what happens in it weatherwise, but much higher up lays the entire universe. We exist smaller than a speck of dust on a living room knick-knack in comparison.

On Ideal Personality 05/20/2024 11:39 AM

Perfection is overrated.

On Paths Unknown 05/21/2024 02:00 AM

We are stuck in this world for unknown reasons. I hope you can make it the rest of the way without too much difficulty. A Celtic tune I hear.

On Science Gods 05/21/2024 11:40 AM

Just how fracking stupid is this world? Biology can't be supplanted by mangled words alone. Mangled bodies, yes. Mangled words, no. Science!

On Novel Writing 05/22/2024 02:54 PM

Life has a known biological beginning and an unknown biological ending.

On Poor Travels 05/23/2024 01:17 PM

It's okay to feel lost sometimes, but not okay to feel lost all of the time.

On Playing Games 05/25/2024 12:17 AM

Ready, set, go away.

On Playing More Games 05/25/2024 12:19 AM

Take your marks, get set, never mind.

On Love Pickles 05/25/2024 02:04 AM

Love takes a while to come alive but can end in a heartbeat.

On "Phase" 05/25/2024 08/29 PM

An old man falls asleep, then finds himself in a large cavern of several rooms. He learns from ceiling hung neon lights, flashing fast, he must choose three assistants to help him escape the cavern amidst eight cubicles inhabited by beings and creatures who appear human-like. The cubicles are only about 5 feet in height. He can't tell if the creatures are sitting or standing. He walks around the cubicles, but no entryways are apparent. Neither hazards nor benefits of his choices appear visible for analysis. No audio sounds intercede on his behalf. The inhabitants of the cubicles appear motionless. He's hungry, and his first fight is to ignore such a bodily distraction.

On Human Priorities 05/26/2024 03:20 PM

In the age of ever-increasing virus multiplications and manipulations, I'm surprised no pill or drink has been created to self-stimulate an orgasm or ejaculation in humans. (Tip back the cup and up, up, and away we go.) (Warnings: extended use may cause heart disease and significant stroke risks. Not advised for use while driving or cycling.)

<u>On Government Classes</u> 05/27/2024 07:21 PM

At the rate of change in many countries, the middle class will be mafia-style rubbed out by the government class.

<u>On Speech</u> 05/29/2024 07:47 PM

PC (Politically Correct) has evolved into Woke (-A-Dope) and now morphed into RC (Ridiculous Crapola).

<u>On Speech Parameters</u> 05/30/2024 02:34 PM

The search for enlightened sentience in this portion of the 21st century has more than rivaled the same search that began more than six decades ago. Big Tech has constructed a maze full of traps (marketing ads galore) and dead ends (totalitarian format and usage pronouncements) to assist further a chaotic search effort.

<u>Third-Eye Sight</u> 06/01/2024 09:14 PM

Some people can still see with their eyes closed. Of course, some people cannot see even with their eyes opened.

<u>On Solemnity Moments</u> 06/02/2024 01:21 PM

When the mind is actively relaxed, the heart brings thanks.

<u>On Computer Seas</u> 06/02/2024 01:25 PM

Passwords come and go like the brine cleansing a sea.

<u>On AI Contributions</u> 06/02/2024 01:35 PM

AI is a birth of the human mind. How has the human mind worked out for this world? Some good, some bad, but ultimately misery and destruction results consistently.

<u>On Ado</u> 06/07/2024 02:57 AM

Much ado about something.

<u>On Upside Downed</u> 06/07/2024 02:13 PM

It's quite odd in the 21st century that we all have to become good citizens in order to be considered terrorists by the government.

<u>On Governance</u> 06/07/2024 02:19 PM

Governments reflect the citizens and their illegals.

<u>On Government Sludgers</u> 06/08/2024 02:50 PM

It's typical of government politicians to take away as much wealth as they can get away with to prevent citizens from financially defending themselves. The tipping point in such a corrupt scale balance has been reached and far exceeded. The morals of citizens have evolved much also, as another self-defense mechanism. See how many government workers exist now, many times in number than ever before, except perhaps during WW2.

<u>On Cities and Citizens</u> 06/11/2024 10:39 AM

If you're wondering what a citizen is like in a city, just look at their city. It is a mirror image of the soul.

<u>On Belief Resilience</u> 06/11/2024 11:41 AM

Tell me what to believe and I will ask why you believe it, as long as my "why" is still considered legal. A doubt persists in me.

On Truth Contraindications 06/11/2024 05:30 PM

For some, the truth will set them free. For some, the truth will crush them.

On Thinking Assists 06/12/2024 01:07 PM

Armchair elbow seems a thing. I've noticed my left arm elbow sports a reddish round rough patch. Guess I only just noticed after a long thinking patch during latest book writing.

On Gods 06/12/2024 09:53 PM

Anyone wonder why human created gods treat humans and all creatures like snot detritus?

On Writing 06/13/2024 11:17 AM

There's always a method to the madness. Just have to perfect the former (method), then wrangle the latter (madness).

On Varied Voices 06/14/2024 01:32 AM

His voice, to me, sounded like the first few breaths ex-post masturbation cycle conclusion. Wise in sound yet satisfied in style. The long night leaked into pre-dawn morning.

On Wisdom's Redux 06/15/2024 01:59 PM

No new social wisdom has been discovered in over a thousand years.

On Negative Needs Seeds 06/15/2024 03:04 PM

Who wants what? When, where, why, and how? Does it really matter?

On Labels 06/15/2024 03:38 PM

I guess the opposite of ne'er do wells is ne'er do ills.

On Promised Obligations 06/16/2024 12:31 AM

A big fear is leaving too soon, before all necessary obligations are completed.

On Perfect 06/16/2024 12:51 PM

Perfection is an illusion.

On Time Passages 06/17/2024 01:55 PM

When younger, each day passes like a month in time. When older, each month passes like a day in time.

On City Decay 06/17/2024 01:59 PM

Many parts of cities have evolved into shit dumps and misery traps.

On Music 06/17/2024 03:01 PM

In many emotional times, the music helps to carry a spirit onward.

On Confidence 06/17/2024 03:28 PM

Sureness involves a temporary mind imbalance. Reduction of a creatures self-defense system.

On Fear 06/17/2024 03:49 PM

A rational fear strengthens the mind. An irrational fear erodes it. The boundary separating these intellect lands is anything but apparent.

On Desires and Desires Not 06/18/2024 02:28 AM

The body is not up to it whether the mind is or not.

On Word Webs 06/18/2024 03:05 PM

Find a fancy word, then crush it with a rock.

<u>On Fiscal Responsibility</u> 06/19/2024 01:11 PM

We don't need more taxation. We do need more budget cuts. If citizens elect crooks, then the citizens are conspirators in the crookery mill production process.

<u>On Corruption Jealousy</u> 06/19/2024 01:14 PM

The leftists are jealous of the criminal classes.

<u>On Governments and Media</u> 06/19/2024 01:51 PM

We need an honest government. We don't need a corrupt government. We need an honest media. We don't need a corrupt media.

<u>Bodily Function Poem</u> 06/19/2024 03:15 PM

Gotta piss. Gotta piss. Gotta piss, piss, piss.

Surely hoping for never a miss.

The landing spot is moving.

Or are fingers gently grooving?

Odds seem good, tinkles should.

Hit the spot inside, not out.

Sorry, poor tile floor grout.

(Where the hell did that come from?!?)

<u>On Government Etiology</u> 06/20/2024 04:29 PM

Governments always and without fail evolve into worst case scenario totalitarian monsters, then begin a slow degradation of control and power.

<u>On Big-Tech Revelations</u> 06/20/2024 08:25 AM

Big-Tech taught us this world is much crazier of mind than we realized.

<u>On Sexual Contracts</u> 06/21/2024 03:39 PM

There is a cost for spreading sexual seeds. Obligations tend to sprout. Negotiations required before the transaction is sealed involving mental, physical, and spiritual elements.

<u>On Journalism</u> 06/24/2024 03:31 PM

Journalism is dead. Journalists have richly proved themselves as nothings. Just useful idiots.

<u>On Judgment Day</u> 06/26/2024 12:59 AM

The civil case filed against the Universe is dismissed on Summary Judgment grounds for failure to state a claim upon which dark matter relief can be granted.

<u>On Fudging the Mustard</u> 06/26/2024 02:32 PM

A good place to write "The End".

<u>On Post Scripts</u> 06/26/2024 02:52 PM

Syntax works like a sin tax.

Reviews appreciated.

Books by Mike Gutowski

(available on Amazon.com as paperback or e-book)

Cratch

Time for the Dead: Zombies-A Love Story

Ariadne

Misfortunes Of Mister Knack

Seventh Ratica

According To Helen

www.ingramcontent.com/pod-product-compliance
Lightning Source LLC
Chambersburg PA
CBHW071154300726
48975CB00004B/1153